Down & Dirty

Tess needs a spanking. She really, really needs a spanking. She needs it so bad that she's wet under her skirt; her pussy is swollen and tight, aching and hungry to feel the sting on her ass as she shakes back and forth, sobbing and crying. She needs it so bad she keeps messing up, bringing me the wrong file, the wrong document, spilling my coffee, forgetting the cream.

But I don't need an excuse to spank Tess—

Down & Dirty

69 super sexy short-shorts

edited by
Alison Tyler

Pretty Things Press

Down & Dirty
Copyright 2003 by Pretty Things Press
all stories copyright 2003 by the respective authors
All Rights Reserved
Cover Design: Eliza Castle

First Pretty Things Press Edition 2003

First Printing 2003

ISBN 1-57612-190-9

Manufactured in the United States of America
Published by Pretty Things Press
www.prettythingspress.com

98765432

"Is sex dirty? Only if it's done right."
—Woody Allen

Introduction

Introduction

Everyone has the potential to be dirty. You might think you're incapable of diving into the naughty side, of crossing over from simply creative to seriously kinky. And yet, if put in the right (or wrong) situation, you can fool even yourself. Trust me. I know. I thought I was good. I thought I was nice and sweet and honest. And then I met Eden.

Eden was exactly my age. He was strikingly handsome, so handsome that strangers would turn around for a double-take when they passed by him on the street. He worked in the cafe at my building, and he sent me sexy smiles whenever I went to buy coffee. I wasn't supposed to like him. Despite his smiles. Despite the fever-flush of total arousal I felt whenever I looked his way, when I brushed his hand, when I kissed him, when he pressed me up against the wall behind the building and fucked me—

I wasn't supposed to like him because I was already taken. Seriously taken. *Engaged* taken.

Still, I fell. Fell hard and fast and down and dirty. Fell into the back seat of his bright red Cadillac, fell into his arms, fell onto the floor of his apartment. And I have to say that I liked it. Who am I kidding? I fucking loved it. When you're clean—when you're innocent and sweet and smile all the time and say "please" and "thank you" in that polite, humble way...well, you don't know what dirty is.

But I know now. And I've never gone back.

After you read the down-and-dirty selections in this arousing anthology, you won't want to go back either. You'll be addicted. Not specifically to cheating, perhaps, (although some pieces, such as "Like a Virgin for the Very First Time" by Maxim Jakubowski and "Package Deal" by Alex Reed *do* deal with extra-curricular erotic activities) but addicted to breaking boundaries in general. To following your carnal needs and discovering each dirty little secret hidden within your libido.

The short stories in this collection—and they *are* short, no more than 2,000 words apiece—are written by the best authors in the business, including M. Christian, N. T. Morley, Thomas S. Roche, Sage Vivant, and Rachel K. Bussel. Some are sensational sexual snippets, others fully detailed dramatic depictions. Featured in this gathering are stories about spanking, tickling, menage a trois, public sex, bondage, girls with girls, phone sex, sex toys, and more. While the themes range across any X-rated connoisseur's favorite lustful laundry list, all of the pieces have one thing in common: They're dirtier than dirty.

Which, I gotta admit, is exactly the way I like them.

Your unruly editor,
Alison Tyler

Yes

by Dante Davidson

"When I get you home, I'm going to spank that beautiful ass of yours until you can't sit down—"

"Home—" Sandrine interrupted, tilting her head at him, dark auburn curls falling away from her sun-kissed face. "Back in New York? So that must mean I get to be naughty until then. Two more full days of out-and-out naughtiness."

James looked at her with his sternest expression in place. "The hotel," he said, amending his prior statement. "And you just made life even harder on yourself, baby doll. You just won your perky ass an extra ten strokes."

"*This* ass?" Sandrine asked, slipping sideways in the seat and rubbing one hand over her ripe, round curves. Her husband took his eyes off the road just long enough to admire her gorgeous rear view, and he gave her one playful swat before she could slide back into the proper position.

"You know it," he said. "You know exactly what it's going to feel like, don't you, Sandy? Spread over my lap, that sinfully short white skirt up to your waist, your panties pulled down—"

"Panties?" she asked next, and then she started to lift the hem of the Lycra skirt up in front, slowly, so that he'd get a view of the increasing yardage of her naked thighs above her stockings and garters. "Which panties?" she asked next, and he caught a glimpse of her cleanly waxed pussy lips, dotted with a decadent design done in shimmering rhinestones. Since arriving in California, his girl had gone totally native, even indulging in the latest sexy looks for the region between her thighs.

"That just makes things easier for me," he grinned at her. "Doesn't it?"

"Easier—" she repeated, having as much fun with this game as he was.

"When I paddle that ass of yours. Nothing to get in the way."

Sandrine loved when he talked to her like that. Suddenly, she didn't think she could wait the twenty minutes it would take to get to the hotel before fucking him. When she told James this, he gave her a lecherous smile. "*You* don't have to wait, do you?" It was all the encouragement she needed to reach over, unbuckle his belt, and free him from his slacks. With a graceful motion, she bent at the waist and locked her ruby-glossed lips around the head of his knob, then brought the first inch into her mouth. James sighed at the sensation, and at his response she got even wetter, knowing that she was pleasing him. He wrapped one hand in her long hair, helping her find a rhythm that he liked.

"Oh, fuck," he moaned, "that is so good."

Sandrine kept slurping at the encouragement, flicking her tongue around James's tool, then working her lips in an even tighter, more ferocious embrace. James gave her cock-sucking lessons as she worked. "Lick it," he said, his voice gone low and deep, "from the tip to the base of the shaft. Work for it, girl. Really reach for it."

Sandrine used the flat of her tongue to follow his instructions precisely. She wanted to get him off before they arrived at their hotel—this was her personal mission. If she was going to work, then he would have to work, too. Work at keeping his mind on the road while his libido shot upward into the stratosphere.

"Now give it a nice, wet kiss," he said, sounding pleased. "I mean, really sloppy."

Sandrine got her lips wet with a lick of her tongue and then French-kissed the head of his cock. It seemed to kiss her back, his pre-come flavàring her mouth. She savored the sensation, enjoying the taste of him for a moment before continuing to service his throbbing member.

"You've sucked cock before," he said, voice hoarse, pushing her head down as he climaxed. Now, she swallowed hard, taking every drop deep down her throat.

Her cunt was sopping and she truly couldn't wait to feel his cock inside her. She looked around, wondering if there was a place for them to pull over, just as they arrived in the circular driveway of the Four Seasons. Perfect timing.

The couple left the rented car with the valet, then hurried through the lobby to the elevator, and when the doors closed, Sandrine got on her knees again, ready to take him into her mouth. He was already hard again. She could see that from the tent in his pants. James had another idea. The compartment was walled with mirrors, and he told her to stand up, then turned her so that she was facing her reflection. Quickly, he lifted her skirt, parted her lips, and dipped his still-wet cock into her dripping pussy.

"You like that?" he asked.

The mirrors bounced their reflections from wall to wall, so that she and James were fucking to infinity. Sandrine forced herself to keep her eyes open wide for the whole ride. It was difficult. She wanted to squeeze her eyelids closed as the pleasure intensified. Besides, watching herself on the verge of orgasm was a little disconcerting. Her eyes had a bright light in them, and her lips were parted with a hungry, yearning expression.

As always, James was more in control of himself. His face remained composed as his cock slid easily in and out of her pussy, making those sexy wet noises as he glided in her juices. His balls slapped against her with each thrust, and he easily lifted her off her feet to give himself better leverage. Sandrine loved the feeling of being wrapped in his great strong arms, his mammoth prick filling her up inside, and she sighed with disappointment when the car reached the top floor. James quickly slid out of her and readjusted his clothes. Then he picked her up, threw her over his shoulder, and carried her to the suite.

When they reached the door, he punched in the code, opened the knob with one hand, and carried her inside. From this position, her skirt had ridden up, revealing her bare ass, clad only in a garter belt. James gave her bottom a hard smack, and she made a happy sighing noise to let him know how much she liked it.

"All bad girls should have their bottoms spanked," James told her, sitting down and quickly positioning his wife over his lap. She could feel his rock-hard cock pressing up against her from below, and she squirmed on it, hoping that he would enjoy the friction. "And you are a bad girl, aren't you?"

Right on the verge of a spanking, Sandrine's mind generally stopped working. Her thoughts were busy focused on the sparkling pain in her immediate future, and the undeniable pleasure that would follow. Fear tinged the entire episode, because she didn't know if James was going to make his previous statement come true. Would he really spank her so hard that she'd have trouble sitting? When she realized that he was doing nothing, just waiting, she understood that he expected an answer.

It took her a moment to mentally replay his question:

Was she a bad girl?

She knew the correct answer by heart, knew what to say in order get exactly what she wanted. A simple, single word: Yes.

The Professor and Marianne
by Sage Vivant

"You can pick up the notes from one of the other students, Marianne," Professor Morrissey said brusquely. "It was the class on illegal searches and seizures."

She hadn't come to his office after hours to be so easily dismissed.

"I can't rely on other students. That's why I came to you."

He looked up from his desk finally, his sloe-eyed stare piercing her with dark curiosity. She flashed him the smile she knew was her most devastating.

"I'm particularly interested in strip searches," she continued, tossing her wave of blonde hair back over her shoulders to reveal her braless breasts under the clingy white top. Even before she touched a finger to a nipple, she knew it was hard.

"Marianne, I don't think this is the appropriate—"

She tilted her head, still smiling as she stroked the gentle slope of her full breast. "What's not appropriate? Searches? Seizures? College students who need help?"

"You know what I'm talking about. You shouldn't be touching yourself in front of me that way." His gaze kept returning to her voluptuous chest.

"Why? Does it make you hard?"

She'd never seen skin as dark as his blush, but there it was—a deepening of his color as he blinked nervously. "Please stop."

"If I were a criminal, what kind of search would be legal?" She worked herself from the front of his desk to his side. Once there, her free hand played with the hem of her very short skirt. He watched cautiously.

"Better yet," she continued, "I'd love for you to show me what's *illegal*." Grabbing a handful of skirt at her crotch, she raised it to reveal a smoothly shaved pussy. Her juices had already started to spread to the insides of her thighs.

His hands trembled and he now stared at her with an appealing mix of confusion and desire. She wanted to help him as much as she wanted to toy with him. She slid a finger over her clit and pushed it between her swollen pussy lips. "I feel certain this would be prohibited by law," she whispered.

With great effort, he got to his feet, using the desk for support. "Get on the desk." She complied immediately, and as he helped her climb on top of the desk, he let one hand cup a luscious breast while the other sampled her dripping pussy. He positioned her so that her ass stuck up in the air, begging for a spanking. He slid her tiny skirt up over her shapely behind to expose her completely.

After fingering her slippery folds until her moans were constant, he slapped her rounded globes gently. She felt her skin ignite under his touch.

"You're a naughty girl, Marianne. Making me want to fuck you right here in the classroom."

His warm, sensitive hands traveled over her body with a slow hunger. When his cock plunged into her wet, waiting hole, she gasped and threw her body into his thrusts, forcing him deeper inside her.

She felt certain this was all wonderfully illegal.

Like a Virgin
for the Very First Time
by Maxim Jakubowski

It never was better than the first time. Later occasions might prove more sensual, longer, more kinky or perverse, more skilful or lasting, technically outstanding or just proficient, but it just wasn't the same.

And every first time in initially unknown hotel rooms was the best of all.

Years later, when the thrill of the chase had faded, or when he just couldn't find the mental energy within his soul to embark on yet another transitory relationship that could only tread a road to nowhere, he would swim willingly through the reef of memories and vicariously treat himself to a movie of past, long-gone moments, secure in the knowledge that those times would never be his again to taste, enjoy, experience, struggle with. It would be like a private library, a unique collection where sensual, tender memories would rival the space customarily devoted by the collector within to books, CDs and DVDs. A scintillating gallery of moments, of mental impressionism.

A hotel room near an airport where no one was likely to recognize them, the smell of ozone in the air and the distant rumbling of jumbo jets on their approach or departure: that indefinable feeling of burning up inside because the lust is just accumulating at a rate too fast for the heart to burn it off like mere calories, the nagging fear of the unknown, the unusual surroundings of the hotel room. This is what they have been building up for three agonizing months of on/off/on/off/on debates in city bars, 'do we sleep together or don't we?' A tentative kiss.

Her mouth is warm and soft. As ever. The look in her eyes. Pleading. Scared. Eager. Submissive. Defiant. They have wife and husband back home, in ignorance.

Their first infidelity.

Adultery set loose that would change their lives forever.

His hand, finally, moving to her body, the pliant elasticity of her thigh. The undressing. The foreplay and, like a holy proclamation half an hour later, her cry of need: "I want you inside me now...." The first time he fucked Kate. The way her brown eyes watched his every movement and thrust inside her. Her sounds. The white alabaster landscape of her body and the scarlet tinge of the orgasmic flush that sometimes overcame her shoulders and chest. Memories that can never be erased.

Then, a hotel in Amsterdam, overlooking a grey canal and parked bicycles. The awkward and slow rise of the elevator up to his floor, following their furtive, eyes down, passage by the night porter's desk and an endless walk through the redlight district, both knowing that they are going to end up in bed, but delaying the inevitable on and on. The frantic fumbling for each other's lips and hands roaming freely over willing bodies, the tugging of clothes. He gets on his knees and slowly, in the semi-darkness, pulls her panties down. Her pubic hair is all curls and slightly damp. He sniffs, but all he can smell is the remote fragrance of soap. He inserts a finger inside her cauldron. She is on fire. She moans. He quickly pushes her back against the bed and she allows herself to collapse with languor over the drawn bed cover. He is hard as hell and almost bursting with a rage to tear her apart, this soft-spoken girl with the lovely accent. She is already so wet. He remembers a past conversation and guides her around on to her knees, her stated preference to be taken doggie-style. She angles her rump towards him. The view of her exposed openings is like a salutary slap in the face, unforgettable, powerful, indelibly obscene. He moves into her in one swift movement, all the while storing the memory in the safety of his grey matter.

Or, again, this time a hotel in Paris, with exposed wooden beams crisscrossing the ceiling and far wall. He has barely known her a month or so and their first meeting in the flesh, so to speak, was at the railway station just an hour ago. Their only contact prior to today was by e-mail or telephone. It's a crazy situation but it somehow makes complete sense. She was so much taller than he had expected but her breasts are a wonder to behold. Fingers, lips and feelings have already played a mad dance of lust and their clothes are in disarray. "Wait," she says and rises, divine areas of flesh exposed, and tiptoes quickly to the bathroom. A few minutes later, she returns. She is quite naked. He holds his breath back as he stares at the smooth, shaven area of her cunt. Of course, he already knew, not only had she told him but his exploratory fingers some minutes ago had certainly double-checked, but the vision is just too much. He feels as if his heart has stopped. She signals for him to lie down and her mouth envelopes him. He has to think of books and such to avoid coming inside her throat prematurely. Shortly after, she confesses she loves him. Lust and feelings, an unholy mix, just like romanticism and pornography.

The safety of unknown hotel rooms, as anonymous as internet forums or chat lines. The cozy coexistence of unbridled sexual excess and mundanity. The rooms, the women, the acts.

They say that, at the moment of death, your whole past parades in front of your eyes, like a film on a loop, fast, out of control, out of reach.

He sometimes wonders whether, when the moment finally comes, his own epiphany will be full of hotel room horizons and beautiful fucks.

He hopes it will.

All Eyes On Her
by M. Christian

The city sat around her. From where she was standing, nothing but the silver squares of windows seemed to be watching. But she knew better; she could feel them sitting behind their desks, in their living rooms, in the bedrooms, in their beds, watching her.

The gravel and tar paper of the roof was hot underfoot, but she enjoyed it. It was the totality of it, the completeness of the act, that made her nipples into hard knots and stoked the fire of her cunt. Wearing slippers, shoes, or anything else would've made it incomplete, would've ruined the statement: standing naked on the rooftop, letting the city watch her.

At first Cindy didn't think she could do it. This was a private thing, something to lay back in a warm tub and think about—rubbing herself into a rolling orgasm. In the real world the roof was hot, the gravel hurt the bottoms of her feet, and a hard wind cut over the concrete edge of the roof and blasted through her.

Despite the pains in her feet, the chill air, and the hot tar, she stood naked on the roof of her little five-story apartment building, a fire roaring in her cunt.

There, that little square: he watched her. Slowly, he got harder and harder till all of his few inches was strong and hard in his hand. He watched, smiling, happy and excited. When he came, he selflessly groaned, and got his window messy.

Cindy watched the city watching her. Looking at one silvery window in particular she lifted her right hand to her left breast and stroked the soft skin and pinched the hard nipple.

—*they watched her. Taken with her brazenness, the attitude of this obvious species of urban nymph, who could say who started it? Maybe it was Michelle who first dropped her shorts and started the kiss. But then it could've been Stacie who started it, who put her hand between them to feel her own growing arousal. Was it Michelle who dropped to her knees and started to lick Stacie's clit?*

Or was it Stacie?

Who came first?

Did Stacie buck against Michelle's mouth? Or did Michelle push fiercely against Stacie's face? Or did it really matter? The end certainly justified the means—

Cindy looked up at the sun. It bathed her, baked her; her skin vibrated with the heat of it, the fire it coated her with. Right hand still on left, she felt her breast, playing with the texture of it, the underlying muscle, the strong tip of her nipple. Sun on her, she moved left to right, massaging her breasts under the gaze of the warm sun.

—sitting on their bed, she watched the woman on the rooftop across the street. The sun was almost too bright, too hot, and for a moment she thought about what she had to do: shower, get dressed, go to work. But the woman, the daringness of her, the casualness of her, kept her glued to the window. She didn't seem crazy, but that's what she had to be. To stand up there in the sight of God and everyone else, and rub herself like that. It turned her on something fierce. It made her horny, that's what it did. She savored the word as she pulled herself up from sitting to all fours. Her breasts pulled away from her body in this position—they strained against her body and rolled in her house dress.

Without thinking, she put a hand down the front of her dress and cradled one of her breasts. The nipple was so hard, it ached, it was so hard. Cautiously, she squeezed and pulled gently at it. Fire raced through her. Her legs felt like they were going to collapse. The woman across the street, touching herself, it was like she was crazy, touching herself and thinking about her nipples and between her legs she could feel herself grow wet—

Her legs were tired, so Cindy lowered herself down till she squatted over the hot gravel roof. Her breasts were heavy and tight, her nipples ached to be touched and sucked. No thought. Not a one. Watching the city watching her, Cindy put a hot hand between her hot legs. Her thighs were wet, her cunt was a damp forest of blond curls. Her lips were wet and hot. She ran a single finger from her clit to her cunt to her ass, and shivered in delight.

—bent over the chair, her ass in the air, her arms down the chair back, her knees on the seat, Betty could feel Bob's tongue playing with her

cunt. He loved to eat her, and, God, he was good at it. She pushed herself back towards his face, trying to get his hard, strong, tongue deeper into her soaking cunt. Then he found her puckered asshole, and started to tongue around it. Christ! She felt like screaming. She needed cock now, right now in her soaking pussy, she needed to be filled, fucked, she wanted to come and come and come! Then Bob was at her clit, and the world seemed to boil down to the points of her nipples, the glow of her ass, the wetness of her cunt, her lover's tongue, and the joy of her clit. She was so lost, so incredibly lost getting ready to come, that she almost forgot to look up, to look across the way to see what that chick on the roof was doing next—

Cindy's cunt juice ran between her fingers. She was so wet. Her cunt was soaking, her clit was a hard bead between her legs, tucked between her lips. She'd worked out a system, and it was working real good: first she'd plunge her hands deep within herself, up and deep till she could swear THERE was her G-spot. Then she'd pull out, slow and hard, pushing aside her hot, soaking lips till her fingers glided past her clit. Then she'd work it, rubbing around and around the little bead of her clit. Then back—back to her cunt, the depths of her, her hot lips, her clit, over and over again.

Sometimes she'd use both hands, pushing all fingers into herself like some huge cock. Sometimes she'd use just one, saving the other, wet and smelling of her cunt, on the knots of her nipples, her aching breasts.

Then she came, fast and oh-so-hard, with the whole world watching.

Left Out

by Lillian Alexander

Sara wished she'd been invited. She knew all of them well enough so that she could visualize the person to go with each laugh she heard, tinkling up to her from the balcony below.

There. That was the school teacher, second grade, she recalled, at Jordan Elementary on the corner of Main and Fourth. And there. *That* was the woman from the flower store, the owner, small with a dark bob. She often smiled to Sara when she walked past the shop on the way to her bus, but Sara rarely met the woman's gaze. It was too inquisitive, too intrusive.

The next voice belonged to the hostess of the party, a dancer. Sara had seen her long legs flash in the pool, body clad in a somber black maillot. The dancer never dressed in dark clothes to go out, always wore bright colors: red, purple, a brilliant blue cashmere coat that nearly brushed the ground when she moved.

Sara walked to the balcony of her own apartment, built—she knew—exactly like the one below, like all the ones on this side of the building. She imagined that the dancer stood directly beneath her, with one foot turned out in a classic pose, and a glass of chilled white wine in her hand. The dancer had her head thrown back as she laughed at a joke told by, who . . . the boyfriend, of course, a great tall man with reddish blonde hair and enormous arms that bulged with muscles.

But why hadn't Sara been invited?

She wasn't that much older than the rest of them, younger, in fact, than a few. And she didn't appear that stand-offish, did she? There was more laughter, loud enough that Sara thought it would drive her mad. She considered calling the police, reporting a disturbance. Then a more daring thought occurred to her. Quickly, without pausing to give herself time to back out, she put on her best black dress. She fixed her hair and touched up her makeup. Just as quickly, she walked down the stairs to apartment 4E and tried the knob. The door opened and Sara walked in, hoping to blend quietly with the others.

Instead, there was a sudden silence. Sara stood, her hand still on the door, and felt the eyes of the rest of the partiers focus on her. The other people were all naked. Every one of them. They were in various positions around the room. Some were in the middle of actually having sex, others were simply leaning against each other, kissing. Or talking. But *all* were naked. Sara, in her black evening dress and black hose, was a striking figure against the various colors of skin.

"I..." Sara started, but then she realized she had nothing, absolutely nothing to say. She was barging in, uninvited, and so was unable to act horrified. But how *should* she act?

The hostess of the party, Serina, who was entangled with one of the other guests on the chaise lounge, smiled at Sara. "I'm so glad you could join us," the dancer said, her smile smeared with the glistening juices of her lover's pleasure. "I didn't know if you'd be interested in attending one of our get-togethers. But now that you're here, please make yourself comfortable."

A striking redhead, about Sara's height and size, moved closer to the doorway. The woman, whose pussy was covered with a fur slightly lighter then her shoulder-length mane, seemed to understand Sara's desire to flee.

"My name's Elaine," the redhead said. "Why don't you come with me to the bedroom. You might feel more comfortable undressing there."

Undressing? Sara's eyes grew wide. But then, because she had been left out her whole life, because she'd never done anything risque at all, she followed Elaine down the hall. Elaine's ass was round and firm and Sara was captivated by it as she entered the bedroom. Once inside, Elaine waited, patiently, for Sara to disrobe. Sara took a deep breath, then undressed. Naked, she stood with her arms awkwardly at her sides and stared at Elaine.

The redhead smiled, winningly, and motioned toward the bed. "Would you like to join me in here? It might be less intimidating at first then joining the party right away."

Inwardly, Sara sighed with relief. She let Elaine lead her to the bed, where they both sprawled on top of the coats and clothing of the rest of the partiers. Sara felt a fur coat beneath her ass, and she liked its soft tickle. Then, as Elaine purposefully parted her legs and used her thumbs to part Sara's pussy lips, Sara learned that she liked the soft tickle there, as well.

She couldn't believe that only minutes before she'd been feeling sorry for herself, alone in her apartment. Now, there was this sparkling beauty making sweet love to her delta of Venus, in a way she'd never had anyone make love to her, on a bed lined with mink and silks and satins. Sara sighed and closed her eyes, basking in the glow of Elaine's knowing ministrations.

Suddenly, she felt something brushing her lips. She opened her eyes to find herself staring into Elaine's pussy. The cunning redhead had swiveled her body around so that her mouth was still glued to Sara's cunt, but her own nether regions were in close proximity to Sara's mouth.

It had been an evening filled with revelations. Thinking this, Sara opened her mouth and pressed forward, tentatively, with her tongue, just gently tapping it against Elaine's pussy lips. Elaine responded by moving back, rocking her hips toward Sara's mouth. Sara kept her tongue poked out, stiff, and Elaine impaled herself on it. Empowered by Elaine's hungry groans, Sara swirled her tongue around in Elaine's pussy, bumping up against Elaine's pussy walls, trying to find her clitoris. Sara's had been located swiftly by Elaine, who was now generously bestowing wet kisses to it, and to the sensitive area around it.

When, by simple exploration, Sara found Elaine's clit, Elaine responded deliciously, groaning loudly, pressing her face even more firmly to Sara's wet cunt. The vibrations of Elaine's voice worked within Sara, echoing within the walls of her vagina, and she lifted her hips helplessly toward Elaine, not able to stop the rapid bucking rhythm that her body seemed to crave.

Elaine's moans grew louder, and soon, although Sara didn't immediately notice, the door to the bedroom had opened and the dancer, her boyfriend, and two other guests stood watching in rapt attention. When she came, the bed was ringed by Serina's guests. The applause simply added to the height of Sara's orgasm.

Sara, finally opening her eyes and seeing her audience, felt something inside her give way. Some long held beliefs about herself disintegrated, instantly replaced by a new view, a new concept of both herself and the world around her.

The Direct Approach
by Thomas S. Roche

Misty usually favors the direct approach. I guess this was fairly direct, but still allowed for an element of surprise.

I'll admit, it took me a few minutes to figure out what she was getting at. After all, it was 9:00 am on a Saturday morning and I couldn't remember ordering anything by Fed Ex from an address in Wichita. I was just innocently reading my newspaper on the front porch, enjoying the last wispy strains of morning before the sun pumped the temperature into triple digits. Misty is a night person, and was still slumbering torridly in bed as the heat of the summer morning slowly built up.

A van pulled up and a guy in blue shorts exited and walked up the path.

"Package for you," he said.

"Thanks," I said. "I'm not expecting anything. Jeez, Wichita?"

"Maybe your wife, then?"

I looked at the small, oblong package and narrowed my eyes.

"Nope," I said. "It's addressed to me. Thanks."

I returned to the porch, sat at the white metal table and did some tentative shaking of the package—about the size of a thick hardback book, brown cardboard and sealed with plain paper tape. I went into the house for my pocket knife, then slid it under the cardboard and slit the package from end to end. Whatever was inside was bubble-wrapped. I sliced away the bubble wrap and held a wonder of technology in my hand.

It was a vibrator.

You would think a girl of Misty's age would have long ago bought her first vibrator, but for a chick with a voracious sexual appetite, she's a little unusual. She almost never wanks. I'd never experienced such a thing, but she says she's always had a boyfriend, so she never "had" to.

Of course, the first thing I did when I heard that was made

her masturbate for me, but the temptation of those pretty legs spread wide as she rubbed herself, panting, her eyes wide open and pointed at me, was more than I could handle. I interrupted her moment alone with a moment of my own, and we'd never gotten back to it.

The other thing about Misty is that, as she said, orgasms had always come so easy to her she'd never been inspired to explore new and different ways of coming. Her girlfriends all had vibrators, but she'd never "bothered." Such a bother, I told her. Oh, such a bother. She'd blushed.

I can vouch for Misty's orgasms—they're testament to the fact that every woman comes differently. She comes fast and easy, and repeatedly, sometimes coming as many as six or eight times during one of our marathon lovemaking sessions. Any fewer than four just makes her horny. "If I masturbated very often," she once said, "I'd have to quit my day job."

But I suspected there was something else going on—Misty could be shy, in a way. Shy at trying new things, sometimes. Always eager, she nonetheless had a little trouble starting things.

I regarded the vibrator. It was one of those oblong, vaguely phallic ones, but this one had an attached power pack and a clever little dimple at the tip—presumably for cupping over the lucky lady's clit. The accompanying flyer informed me that the Pulso Ultra-Thousand or whatever the fuck it was called was more powerful than any other vibrator on this green planet, and its Pulso-Ultra power could offer ten—yes, ten!—different speeds, styles and pulses. "Choose your pleasure!" the sex carny bellowed. "Or set it on RANDOM and let chance be your mistress!"

It came with batteries. I put them in and tried the thing out—they weren't kidding. Ten—yes, ten!—different speeds. Enough to fill up a long, lazy summer afternoon of sweating on each other. Enough of a reason to go wake up Misty.

Misty sprawled on the bed, the tangled sheet tossed to one side. She sometimes sleeps nude, but last night she'd put on a long threadbare T-shirt and a pair of panties. Maybe she'd anticipated the express delivery of her message in a bottle and become unexpectedly shy.

I took off my robe and climbed onto the bed, setting the Pulsa-SupraWhatchamacalit next to me. I said Misty's name several times to see if she was still asleep. She was out like a light.

I slid onto her with the vibrator tucked behind me, and she started suddenly, mumbled a rapturous "Mrrf" and pressed her butt against my crotch. She clutched my hand and stroked it, saying "Hi."

"Take off your underwear," I told her.

"Why?" she asked.

I started to kiss the back of her neck, and she shivered. My hands pulled up her shirt and slid under, and I felt her nipples harden in an instant as I nibbled at her shoulder.

"Fine," I said. "I'll do it."

If there's one thing I've learned since I met Misty, it's how to get her panties off quickly. She was still more than half asleep as I eased them down her thighs and over her ankles. I missed the hamper by about two inches.

I nibbled her ear, used my tongue to tease that spot at the top of her spine that always makes her go crazy. When I had her just crazy enough to want it, but not crazy enough to be fully awake, I reached behind me and seized the vibrator.

"You're a very naughty girl," I said. "And a sleepy one," I told her, pushing her onto her belly and forcing her legs wide with my knees between hers.

The faint hum of the vibrator coaxed another curious "Mrf?" out of her in the instant before the tip of it touched her clit.

"Oh, oh God!" she gasped. "What are you doing?"

It was on the lowest setting, barely a fizzle of ecstatic energy pulsing out of the double-As. I had pulled the vibe away from Misty's clit, which was, in point of fact, what had elicited the irritated exclamation of "What are you doing?"

"I thought I hurt you," I said.

"As if," she said, grinding her ass up into my crotch again and with Amazonian effort lifting me into the air even though I've got a hundred pounds on her. I guided the vibe back to the cleft at the anterior of Misty's swollen pussy lips, and she started clutching the sheets, ripping the contour right off the mattress on both ends simultaneously.

"Oh, God," she moaned. "Is that a vibrator?"

"No," I said. "It's a Queen Anne credenza. Yes, it's a fucking vibrator. Does it feel good?"

This time, her "Mrf" wasn't at all sleepy. I eased myself onto her, getting onto my knees as she lifted her ass high and presented her pussy to me hungrily. I pressed the tip of the vibe against her clit again and flipped the dial. She gasped and did in the contour sheet once and for all, and a couple of pillows along with it. Her hips began to grind.

"Oh God," she moaned. "It's got more than one speed. What *is* that?"

"As if you didn't know, you tawdry little whore," I said affectionately, turning the dial again and watching Misty's hips explode in a great series of shudders as she came the first time. I eased the tip of the vibe down to her pussy and she gasped as I slid it in and turned the dial.

"What's that?" she whimpered.

"This setting is especially good for G-spot stimulation," I said with the style of a stereo salesman. "At least, that's what the makers of the Ultro-Pulsa-thousand-whatsit tell me. Would you agree?"

"God, I don't know...." she said. Then her words were gone, as I eased the vibe out of her pussy and moved it back to her clit. The clever little dimple at the end fit right over Misty's oversized bud, and as I held the vibe in place her hips started to pump. She came again, gasping for air as I firmly held the toy in place, riding her. She slumped to the bed, her hips pressed tight to the wrinkle-ruined contour sheet. Then, without pause, she lifted her ass—just her ass, not her belly—in this fetching way she has that tells me "Fuck me, you son of a bitch." I mounted her from behind and slid into her as I cupped the toy firmly against her clit. I started to fuck her long and slow, but she was having none of it. Her hips started to piston, and she drew me deeper into her until I was fucking her just as hard as she wanted to be fucked. The whole time, I kept the vibrator right on her clit. I got the hang of it quickly, and when I felt my shy wife's hand over mine, taking over the vibrator, it made it quite a bit easier to lean back and fuck her rapidly, pumping my cock into her as she moaned and writhed, caught between the vibrator and me.

I felt her pussy contracting around my thrusting cock as a third orgasm exploded into her. That was all I could take, and I came hard, deep inside her as I felt the vibrations rumbling through her pubic bone. Then I plucked the vibrator from her grasp and cradled it as I cradled her.

"Where the hell did you find *that*?" she asked, her voice hoarse from moaning.

"As if you didn't know, you saucy tart."

"No, really," she said.

"You didn't order this," I said flatly.

She narrowed her eyes, took the vibe out of my hand, and looked at it.

"You didn't buy it for me?"

"It just came Fed Ex," I said. "Addressed to me."

"Oh, God," Misty sighed. "It's Virginia. I told her I'd never used a vibrator and she was horrified."

"Why'd she ship it to me instead of you?"

Misty glanced from the vibrator to me and back again.

"I guess she wanted to be sure I'd use it."

"We owe her a thank you call," I said.

"Yeah, we do. Later," said Misty, drawing my hand back down toward her pussy. "Later." She kissed me softly, then harder, her tongue teasing mine. She gasped as I flipped the vibrator on and touched it to her clit.

"Later," she moaned softly. "Much, much, much, much later."

The Naughty Nanny
by J. Nelson

It was to the final strains of my favorite Queen song that the call came in. As Freddy Mercury crooned about his Naughty Nanny, my secretary buzzed me about a new job for my security company. An easy one from the sound of it, but you never know in this business. That's what I've learned after five years at the helm. Security. Sounds good, right? Upstanding. Protective. A job to be proud of. But sometimes, it makes me feel so fucking dirty, I can't even stand to look at myself in the mirror.

This new assignment wound up to be one of *those* sort of jobs.

The call was from a lady in the upscale section of town. She wanted video cameras installed in the nursery, so she could check to see how her new nanny was treating the kids. Fine. We get calls like that a lot.

I sent two of my best guys out to install the devices, and when they came back, they had a story to tell. Of course, the lady wanted the cameras to be invisible. That went without saying. But she also wanted the bill to be invisible, meaning that she paid immediately with cash. "Don't want to bother my husband about it," is what she explained to Larry. "Seemed strange," Larry told me. "None of my business, you know. But wouldn't the dad want to be in on the surveillance?"

I just shrugged. I try not to get involved.

"Anyway," Larry said, "you should have seen this piece of ass—"

Now, I looked at him, curious. The woman had sounded icy on the phone. I hadn't imagined her possibly being hot. "Mrs. Miller?" I asked.

"No, the *nanny*—"

"Oh," I nodded, "the nanny."

"Yeah, she was the blonde thing. Tall and lean, long hair, great body. Even just in jeans. She was hot."

I don't know why, but I had a feeling right then. A premonition, I guess, that this job wasn't over. The easy ones, at least the ones that appear easy on the surface, those are generally the jobs to worry about. I've learned my lesson many times over. And I was right.

Next day, Mrs. Miller called again. She sounded insanely snobby on the phone, and I could tell that she was very accustomed to getting her way. That's how she got to me through my secretary. Wouldn't take no for an answer. Turned out, she was having a difficult time with the film and the cameras, and I told her I'd send a man out.

"That's not what I want," she said. "I want the boss. I want you."

Okay, so fine. I had a light day planned. I went myself. I was interested in catching a look at the nanny, I have to admit, and I wanted to see what Larry considered a piece. The lady of the house was exactly what I expected. A washed-out looking brunette with one two many visits to the Botox doctor racked up on her Prada belt. She was also one of those non-mechanical minded people. All she had to do was pop out the cassette and plug it into her viewer. But I did it for her, and what we saw was—well—shocking.

At first, all seemed fine. Lovely nanny, sweet to kids, no yelling, no hitting. And Larry was right. The girl was unbelievably hot. Blonde and Nordic-looking with a body to lay awake at night and dream about. Nothing wrong with her at all, as far as I could see.

"Guess that's it," I said, but Mrs. Miller shook her head.

"I want you to show me how to fast forward it. I want to watch the whole tape in its entirety."

So I showed Mrs. Miller how to fast-forward, and that's when things got interesting. After the kids were asleep in the bed off of the nursery, a man entered the playroom.

"John," the woman murmured, more to herself than to me, and I slowed the tape back to normal speed.

In moments, all became clear in my head. The wife wasn't interested in how the nanny was treating her kids. She was interested in how the nanny was treating her husband. And let me tell you, this was one talented nanny. She treated the man of the house fabulously. Oh, lord, how I would have liked those full lips around my own cock. Within seconds, the nanny was on her knees, head bobbing up and down, and John, lucky bastard, was leaning against the wall with a look of pure ecstacy on his face.

Christ, the girl knew what she was doing.

She had her hand between his legs, cupping him, and she sucked her cheeks in deeply as she swallowed him down. Honestly, I didn't know how long I was going to be allowed to watch this, so I stared hard, drinking in every frame. Mrs. Miller seemed unable to move, to think or to speak. Maybe the Botox had atrophied her brain. In silence we watched the rest of the routine.

After the nanny had gotten John's rod wet with her mouth, she stood and quickly bent over, offering her divine backside to her employer. He was a man after my own heart, quickly flipping up her short floral skirt to reveal a white thong neatly separating her rounded asscheeks. Once he'd pulled this flimsy piece of lingerie roughly to the side, he fingered her pussy, obviously determining whether or not she was ready for him.

She was ready. I could have told him that without checking.

He had his hands on her hips in another instant and pulled her back against his spit-slicked shaft. The camera angle caught the expression on the nanny's face. She looked radiant, deeply lit as if from within. In my head, I heard the strains of the Queen song playing when I'd got the job. Here she was: the absolute definition of a naughty nanny. And what she was doing—man, I wished she were in front of me, bent over with her hands flat on the floor while I took her hard and fast from behind. Or I wished I were in front of her, experiencing a little oral action as her employer rode her from behind. That's exactly what I wished—

When I realized that I was getting aroused, I shifted around and cleared my throat. Time to make a clean getaway. That was for sure. Time to go park my car around the corner and jack off in whatever little bit of privacy I could fine. But the ice queen at my side seemed frozen in place, so we stood there and watched without speaking while the hot-blooded naughty nanny continued her service with a smile.

Try This At Home
by Ayre Riley

Really. I'm serious. Try *this*.

That is, if you're in the mood for a salacious evening. If you're not, skip this advice and move onto something else. But if you are, then try this at home!

Get yourself all dressed up in something deliciously extravagant. You know what I mean. Something made of crimson velvet with pale-petal-pink marabou trim, if you're that sort of girl. Or skin-tight and vinyl if you're a vixen into black. Then pose in front of your mirror as you do your make-up. Really go to town with the mascara and the lipstick. You want your eyes to stand out, and you want your mouth to look full and inviting.

Now, here's the key—don't go out.

I'm not kidding.

Don't even think about going out.

Tonight, you and your man are going to stay in.

Of course, the trick to this particular treat is that you *don't* tell him you're not going out. What you do, is invite him over at a specific time—or if you and your honey live together, then tell him to be ready at a specific time—then spring your X-rated outfit on him. He'll look you up and down in that slow, hungry way of his, that he-lion way, and then he'll shake his head slowly, as if he can't believe his luck. Or as if he can't believe you're planning on hitting the club scene all dolled-up like a tart.

Don't blow your cover. Let him stare. Let him ogle. Let him get all hot and bothered. Then strip him. Do you hear me? Strip him completely out of his clothes until he's naked while you're still dressed sex-queen style. Slide in your favorite CD, something with a heavy, throbbing beat. Then make him sit down on an armless chair and give him a lap dance.

You know the rules, right? You get to touch him, but he can't touch you.

Make sure that he sticks to those rules. Hands at his sides so that he behaves like a good boy. Rules are very important to this game. Remember that. And the thing of it is, you're making all the rules tonight.

Chances are, he won't be able to obey completely. I mean, chances are that his cock will try to touch you, even if he keeps his hands welded to his side. Can't punish the boy for that, can you?

'Course you can. Stand up and stare down at his gorgeous cock. Tell it to behave or you won't kiss it. Then bend on your knees in front of him and let him feel your hot breath against his naked skin. He'll be harder than hard at this point. He'll be doing a passable imitation of steel. So break your own rules now and kiss the head. Just the head. Give it any kind of kiss you like: sweet and chaste, wet and sloppy. He won't complain. I'm telling you that from experience. He won't say a word. He'll be too afraid that any movement will stop the pleasure from continuing—and believe me, he doesn't want that.

When you feel that he's earned it, bob your head once or twice. Go on and do it right. You know how. Remember that you have a goal here. You want the shaft to be nice and slippery wet for when you climb on board. What I'm saying is that you're doing yourself a service here by getting him ready for your sweet pussy. Think about that as you glide your tongue down to his balls and then gracefully bring it back up to the tip. Think about that as you finally pull off your own clothes—or at least as much as you need to in order to expose yourself—and slip your body on top of his.

Now, tell him what to do. If you want him to touch your breasts, or kiss your collarbones, or bite your bottom lip, you tell him. If you want him to firmly hold your wrists together over your head, or grip your hips, or kiss your neck, let him know. He won't let you down. Ride him at your favorite speed. Pump your thighs and work him until you feel your own wetness glossing your inner thighs. Then stand up and have him take his spot behind you. Doggy-style is always best at this junction of the game. Place your palms flat in the seat of the chair, arch those pretty hips of yours, and tell him that you're ready. He'll grip onto you as he slides in deep, and then he'll probably use one hand to pull on your long hair, keeping you in place as he takes control.

It's okay if he takes control now—or if he *thinks* he's in control. Because you're about to come, aren't you? Oh, yeah, you are. You're getting so close. Super closer. So use one hand to tickle your own clit as he fucks you, and as you get closer, start to moan. Let him know it's going to happen. Let him know it's going to happen soon!

Do you have all that? Does it all make sense?

Great—because once you've mastered this, I'll be more than happy to teach you Game #2, which is this: Try this in the back seat of your car. I'm serious. The back seat....

Door to Door

by Jessica Dondershein

Being a door-to-door cosmetic saleswoman isn't easy. More women work out of the home these days, so fewer are around when I stop by. Cosmetics are one of life's pleasures, and these same working women often buy their favorites at the mall, choosing chic, expensive name brands. But I have my own route, my own loyal customers, and I'm happy with them.

Sometimes customers recommend their friends, and I decided to do a few cold calls one afternoon to some of the suggested future customers. My first stop was in the high-end neighborhood of Atherton. I knew in my heart that I wouldn't make a sale as I walked up the cobblestone drive. This lady could afford to bathe in champagne. She wasn't going to want my champagne-scented bath for $6.99. But I'm not a quitter. I walked up the path and rang the bell.

The door was opened for me by an impertinent maid in one of those outfits I thought creatively kinky people wore on Halloween. It had a tiny skirt, puffed out around her by crinolines. She wore a lace apron over the whole thing. All in all, she had on about an ounce of fabric.

"Can I help you?" she asked, looking me over with dark eyes that made me momentarily forget where I was, what my name was, what I was trying to sell.

"I'm here to see Ms. Jackson," I finally managed to tell her.

"She isn't available," the maid said. I thanked her and started to leave. "Would you like to wait?" the woman called out to me. This brought a smile to my lips. I turned back and entered the mansion, following the maid down the long marble hall to a woman's bedroom.

"Shouldn't I wait in the living room?" I asked, looking around at the huge bed, the white rugs, the velvet couches.

The maid shook her head and led me to one of the sofas, then sat across from me on the bed. Smiling, she parted her legs, wider and wider, revealing the fact that she didn't have on panties and she *did* have a beautiful, freshly shaved pussy.

She motioned to me. I took a breath, smelling her fragrance from where I sat, and then (making a quick decision), walked over to the bed, got down on my knees, and began to eat her. She had a rich, dark flavor that I lapped at, and as I worked her, she made the sweetest noises, moaning, pulling open the front of her uniform to paw at her own breasts. I got one hand up there, too, helping her out, pinching her nipples slowly, first one and then the other, brushing them with the ball of my thumb until they stood out hard, like tiny jewels.

I used my tongue and my other thumb on her clit, fanning out my fingers to place two in her pussy and tickling her ass with the other two. She was making a huge wet spot on the bed, but it wasn't my bed. I didn't care. When she asked me to undress, to get on top of her, I hesitated. "When's Ms. Jackson due back?"

"Don't worry," she said again. I took another deep breath, looked at her waiting for me, and stripped, climbing on top of her in a perfect sixty-nine. She had the mouth of an angel, using it just right on my sopping cunt, nipping at my lips, nibbling at my clit until I was rocking my hips hard enough to shake the bed. I returned the treatment in kind, fucking her with my mouth and fingers, biting her thighs, spreading her asscheeks and impaling her with two fingers at once, getting deep in there were she was all warm and wet and sticky. I liked that feeling, fucking her asshole, because as she started to come, she squeezed her asscheeks tight around my fingers, as if trying to milk me.

We came at the same time, came again, and I got off her and sprawled out next to her, panting.

"Wow," she said.

I echoed her, then stood and began to dress.

"Don't do that yet..."

"I don't want to be caught in Ms. Jackson's bed..." I started, very aware of my just-been-fucked appearance.

The smile on her face turned to a laugh.

"I don't mind losing the sale," I said. "But I don't want to get arrested."

She laughed harder, then caught herself and grinned at me.

"Trust me, you won't," she said, peeling off her uniform and tossing it aside. For a moment, she stood, naked, letting me see the whole of her beautiful body as she walked to the closet doors and opened them. Inside, neatly hung, were dozens of different uniforms: maid, nurse, doctor, police officer, naval officer....

She walked back over to me, tossing her hair out of her face and extending her hand. "I'm Veronica Jackson," she said sweetly, "pleased to meet you."

Amore
by Luke Artell

I was eighteen when I went to Italy with my parents. It wasn't altogether a dreamlike trip for the three of us. We ended up getting on each other's nerves at every turn. They were still in the "we can make you do whatever we want" mode and I was in the "like hell you can" mode. In the end, we spent a lot of time apart, sightseeing on our own, which I believe saved everyone's sanity.

It was while doing my best to avoid the folks that I met a raven-haired Italian waitress at the cafe near our hotel. All I knew how to say in Italian was "La Fenicci," which was the name of the hotel, "grazzi" (thank you), "prego" (please), and "San Marco" (San Marco, obviously, the lovely pigeon-strewn square in Venice). The only English word the waitress knew was "Levi's," which she pronounced adorably, "Leveees."

But she smiled at me in a very seductive way, and somehow we made do with our lack of verbal skills. Made do on the bed in my hotel room, her skimpy summer-weight black dress balled up on the dresser, my "Leveees" and white T-shirt in a heap on the floor. We sat on the bed together, stripped completely, her legs over mine as we worked to become entwined like human pretzels. She moaned when I kissed her neck, which is my all-time favorite part of a woman. She let me kiss her neck for what seemed like hours, lingering on the pulse point, spending much time at the base of it, that sultry spot between her collar bones. She had long, dark, straight hair, and she tilted her head way back to let me get at her neck, and her hair tickled my fingers, which were holding onto her back.

I loved her smell. She wore a musky perfume, but she also smelled like the cafe in which she worked. Her skin had the flavor of the coffee that she served, and a bit of the spices that they put in the pasta sauce, and some of the wine, as well, as if she took a drink from some customer's half-empty glass every once in awhile.

She tasted dark and rich, but I didn't get down to her pussy until I spent a good, long time drinking all of the scent and flavor from the skin of her neck, and arms, and belly.

When she lay back on my bed, her hair spread around her head like a blanket, and I would start at the tips of it, running my fingers through it. Then I would work my way to kissing her eyebrows, which were thick and dark and amazingly sexy. Her eyes were the brown of the coffee she served, and she'd close them so that I could kiss the fair translucent skin of her eyelids. She had a strong nose, which I traced over and over again with my fingers, and she had a slight cleft in her chin which I believed would make her a movie star if she came to America with me.

By the time I made my way down to her breasts, she'd be breathing hard, but it wouldn't make me work any faster. I spent time on her nipples, because they deserved my time. I kissed and licked them, held them between my lips and sucked them to make them stand out. They were brown, like milk chocolate, and small, but her breasts were also small, so they suited her.

I worked my way down her ribs, not missing one, to her belly. She had a little belly, a small swell of a belly, even though she was a thin girl. I liked to cup it in my hands, to kiss all around it, and this made her smile. She wasn't self-conscious of her body the way American girls sometimes are. She seemed pleased with the amount of lust and energy I bestowed on each part of her. But each part of her deserved it. Every inch of her was divine.

Her pussy was covered in a thick mat of silky dark hair that I liked to lick. I lapped at her fur with the flat of my tongue, parting her lips at the same time and tickling her between them. She responded delightfully, grabbing at me, pushing me down, demanding (I could understand the tone if not the words) that I satisfy her.

I would do nothing less. I would make her come slowly, specifically treating her to the many ways my tongue could bring her pleasure. I taunted her with nips to her pussy lips between caressing circles of my tongue. I took her bursting clit between my lips and sucked it gently, flicking my tongue between my lips to tap on it, rap on it, until she could take no more and she exploded with orgasm and more liquid than any other woman I'd been with. She ejaculated in my mouth, and her taste was as pleasing as the perfume of her skin. It was my desire, my duty, to make her come as many times as I could.

Supposedly, I'd been brought along on this trip so that I could see the world, appreciate my small status within it. But I felt as if I'd been brought to Venice to learn the geography and topography of this one stunning woman. That was my goal. While my parents viewed every artifact, every ancient edifice, I viewed my waitress from every way I could conceive. Upside-down. Bent over. From behind.

We pleasured each other in many positions, turning topsy-turvy on my bed, head-to-tail, bucking against each other like animals. And near the end of my visit, we stole into the square late at night and made love against the base of one of the ancient statues, kissing and fondling in the white-gold moonlight.

When it was time to part—when, sad though it was, we had to say goodbye in the only way we could—I made love to her a final time, memorizing the lines of her lovely neck. Remembering her taste for eternity. I promised to come back and she promised to visit... at least, I think we did. Grazzi, prego, and San Marco don't get you very far in the language of long goodbyes.

But I did give her my Leveees as a token of my "amore."

The Porn Date
by Rachel Kramer Bussel

I'd had a crush on Scott for almost a year, but thus far hadn't been successful in really catching his attention. He knew me, sure, he even said hello when we saw each other in class, but other than that, I was nothing to him. One day after our Contemporary Film class, where we'd been discussing erotic movies, I heard him and his friends talking about their favorite porno flicks. I was a bit surprised with myself when I jumped right into their conversation and said, "Have any of you seen 'Dirty Angels'?" They all looked at me in shock, but Scott's eyes gave me a pretty thorough once-over before meeting mine and smiling right into them. His stare was magnetic, drawing me to him, and neither of us needed to say much more. It was as if he were seeing me for the first time. His friends ambled away and he put his hand on my arm and asked if I wanted to come over that night to check out his porn collection. I'd been angling for just such an invitation, but while my heart flip-flopped in delight, I just smiled coolly at him and agreed.

That night, I dressed carefully. Even though it was obvious that the entire night was engineered, on both our parts, for us to wind up in bed together, I didn't want to hit him over the head with my eager intentions. I wore a pleated gray skirt, tight white T-shirt, denim jacket, and black stockings and tennis shoes. I completed the outfit with a choker and some red lipstick, grabbed my purse, and headed over to his apartment.

He answered the door and played the gentleman, taking my coat and purse, and offering me a drink. I chose a beer, and then he led me over to the TV case where he kept his videos. I stopped myself from clapping in delightful glee; it was like I'd hit the porno jackpot! One entire drawer featured all porn, the others were devoted to animation and endless hockey and baseball games. Most of my girlfriends had three or four regular movies, tops, and no porn whatsoever, but I guess with boys it's different.

I peered into the case, fascinated by the choices arrayed before me. Some were slick store-bought tapes, with shiny, colorfully lurid boxes, others were plain black tapes that had handmade labels with titles like "Girls Who Suck Cock" and "Anal Sex." My eyes lit up when I saw one I'd heard lots about—the one with the heavy metal rocker and his well-endowed model/actress wife. "Where'd you get this?" I asked, picking it up.

"From a friend, you know, we tape them for each other." I nodded and marveled at the difference between the access guys and girls have to porn, grateful to this well-connected (and hopefully well-hung) guy.

"Let's watch this one," I said with an eager grin.

We settled onto the couch, me cradling my beer, sitting near him but not touching him directly. I was quiet during most of the movie, trying to take in all the scurried sexual activity: sex in the car, sex on a boat, sex in the living room, sex anywhere and everywhere. When the film focused in on her lips closing around his enormous cock, I couldn't take my solitary arousal anymore. With my eyes still on the screen, I reached over and felt for Scott's cock. Sure enough, it was nice and hard. I squeezed it through the fabric of his shorts, squirming as I heard his sharp gasp. I squeezed harder as my hand found its way down to his balls. His own hand wandered over to my lap, creeping up my thigh to the edge of my panties, then reaching underneath. His fingers played with my wetness, teasing me by entering me slightly, then pulling out. I stood up and pushed his hips back against the couch, the video now all but forgotten. I straddled his lap. His cock felt even harder now, pushing through our layers of clothing towards my cunt. I ground myself against him, leaning my head back and feeling the ache inside of me. He pulled me to him, his hands urging my hips closer and closer.

I could hear moaning coming from the TV as I sat up again, leveraging myself against the couch long enough to take my panties off. I rubbed my clit hard and then stuck my first two fingers inside me, slicking them, then put them into his mouth. He suckled them, reveling in my juices. I lifted up my skirt so he could see my pussy.

At that, I could see his cock straining to get inside me, jerking inside his briefs. I stood up and pulled him up with me. I led him into the bedroom, discarding my clothes as I went. I reached the bed and lay down on my stomach, naked, bent over. "Mmm." he said, groaning as his own clothes quickly fell to the floor and his cock jumped forward. He grabbed a condom and I heard him unroll it as I continued to rub my clit, my face pressed into a pillow.

Then I felt the head of his cock pressing into me, and I lifted my ass in the air. He slid into my wet cunt and kept going, filling me as I lifted myself to get closer to him. I relaxed into him, letting myself go. I squeezed his cock as my muscles contracted, and felt myself getting wetter and wetter. He pulled my hair, lifting my head up slightly, and I looked back at him briefly. I knew I was very close to coming. He let go of my hair and leaned forward on the bed, thrusting faster and faster inside me. I rubbed my clit as fast as I could, thinking of Scott, the video, the way his cock felt as he pushed all the way inside me. I felt myself start to come, and gripped the sheets tightly as I shook. I felt shivers move through my whole body. His orgasm followed soon after. He collapsed on top of me, breathing heavily. I smiled.

This had been a *very* successful porn date.

Christmas Morning
by N.T. Morley

Before she even woke up on Christmas morning, Christelle felt that she was alone in the bed. When she opened her eyes and saw the indentation that her lover had left, she rolled over onto his side of the mattress, feeling his lingering warmth and inhaling deeply of his scent. She had forgotten that it was Christmas until after she had realized that she was horny. As thoughts filtered through her mind, she felt the pressure of her stiffening nipples against the sheets, felt the familiar pulse between her legs, a heat and hunger that always came when she wanted sex. She wished Aaron was here against her, climbing on top of her, or perhaps guiding her down under the covers to take his cock in her mouth. She ran her fingers lazily up her thighs and touched her smooth pussy, feeling how wet it was. She rubbed her clit lightly and gasped at the sensation, moaning softly. If Aaron were here, he would fuck her. She wondered where he'd gotten to.

He had been away for more than three weeks, traveling on business while she attended to her own career. In fact, she'd been so busy she'd hardly had any time to think about what she was going to get him. When Aaron had returned home late last night, Christmas Eve, Christelle had been excited to see him and deeply horny from weeks of deprivation. But Aaron had been too tired from his long plane trip to make love, and the two of them had tumbled swiftly into bed and soon were asleep. She could still feel the ache of pent-up desire for her absent lover. She rubbed herself and moaned, very close to coming—but not wanting to get off without him.

When Christelle finally slipped out of the tangled covers and put on her robe, her legs felt weak and her nipples rubbed firmly against the rough terrycloth. She found Aaron sitting on the living room sofa by the Christmas tree, drinking coffee and reading the newspaper. A series of packages wrapped in silver, gold, red, and green had been neatly arrayed in front of the tree. Aaron wore his silk robe, which hung open far enough to show Christelle her lover's lightly furred chest. She went up to him, sat in his broad lap, and cuddled up against that chest, running her fingers over it as she kissed his neck.

"Merry Christmas," he told her. "Ready to open your presents?"

"They're for me?" she asked, feigning innocence. "But I didn't get you anything!"

"Then you'd better open *your* presents, or it'll hardly be Christmas, will it?"

"Promise you're not mad I didn't get you anything?"

Aaron smiled. "Open your presents," he said warmly.

Christelle retrieved the boxes, counting five. She set them next to Aaron in the sofa and sat in his lap again. She loved the fact that Aaron was big enough to sit on. She picked up the smallest box and shook it. She heard the faint rustling of metal—it sounded almost like a chain. A necklace? Unable to stand the suspense, she ripped open the wrapping and took off the top of the glittering gold box. Her mouth dropped open.

"I hope you're not wearing anything under that robe," said Aaron, tugging away the terrycloth as he took the nipple clamps out of the box. He exposed Christelle's nipples and she moaned softly as he fitted the clamps over them. She gasped as the faint throb of pain settled into her. She felt her clit swell to match the sensation in her nipples, and her pussy suddenly felt hot and tight.

"Next present," said Aaron.

Breathing heavily, Christelle picked up the next smallest box and tore off the wrapping. When the box top came off, she stared, wide-eyed, hand at her mouth.

"Here," said Aaron. "Let me put it on for you."

Christelle obediently sat still in Aaron's lap as his big hands drew the thick black leather collar around her throat, buckled it, and clicked the padlock closed. She felt the pressure of the nipple clamps increasing as her nipples hardened still more. Her pussy was beginning to hurt, it felt so swollen and hungry.

"Open the next box, dear," said Aaron.

Christelle obeyed, quickly tearing the silver wrapping and opening the box. She tried to suppress the moan that issued from her lips as she looked into the box.

"Be a good girl," said Aaron. "Stand up and take off your robe."

Christelle stood and slid her terrycloth robe over her shoulders. It fell in a pool to the floor. She leaned forward, closing her eyes. Aaron had to remove one nipple clamp to thread the chain that connected them through the twin openings of the PVC bra. When he told her to turn around, she obeyed, and he fastened the strap tight across her back, making her nipples stand out distended through the tight, tiny openings. He replaced the nipple clamps and nodded toward the next package.

Christelle curled up in Aaron's lap, nude except for the collar, bra, and nipple clamps. The next box was considerably larger. She plucked off the ribbon, tore the gold paper and opened it.

Her heart pounded so hard she could hear it in her ears.

"Bend over," said Aaron.

Christelle could feel herself shaking as she stood up and bent over the coffee table, supporting herself with her outstretched arms. Aaron fitted the enormous dildo into the harness. Christelle was wet to the point of dripping. But this dildo was considerably bigger than any she'd ever taken, bigger even than Aaron's cock. He teased open Christelle's pussy lips and inserted the dildo with a single rough thrust that made her gasp and straighten up.

"I told you to bend over," he growled.

Christelle obediently bent back over, lifting her ass high in the air as Aaron pushed the dildo all the way into her and buckled the harness around her waist and thighs. The harness was fitted with a rubber ridge that pressed very hard against her clit as Aaron cinched the buckles tight. Aaron licked his thumb, and then as he pried her smooth rear cheeks apart, Christelle felt the firmness of pressure circling her exposed anus.

"I had to look everywhere to find one that kept your asshole exposed," said Aaron. "I prefer to keep it exposed whenever possible."

Christelle responded with an inarticulate moan, her body swaying with the sensations of her stuffed-full pussy.

"Next package," said Aaron.

Christelle was frightened and excited at what she might find. She sat in Aaron's lap with great difficulty, every movement of her lower body seeming to press the dildo deeper inside her and make her shiver with sensation. She was very close to a climax, but it wouldn't do to come until she'd opened the last present.

She tore the red-and-green paper and opened the box.

"You know what to do, darling," smiled Aaron.

And Christelle did. Her hands were shaking, she was so turned on. She took out the big bottle of lube and pulled open Aaron's robe, revealing his fully erect cock. She went down on her knees and took it in her mouth, licking up the shaft to the head. Then Christelle drizzled some lube over the head and smeared it down the shaft. Turning around, Christelle held Aaron's cock in one hand and guided it smoothly between her rear cheeks. Aaron took firm hold of Christelle's hips and pulled her down onto him. Her eyes went wide as she was forced down onto Aaron's cock. She could feel the thickness of his shaft pressing deep into her body, rubbing against the fullness of the dildo already penetrating her. Aaron got a good hold of her and wriggled her down more fully onto his cock, until he was thrust as far as he could go into her tight back door.

Christelle was going to come.

Aaron bent her forward very far so he could increase the friction as he guided her up and down on his cock. His eyes narrowed. He pushed Christelle forward so far that she had to steady herself with her hands on the coffee table. Only the head of his cock now remained in her ass, the shaft glistening with lubricant. Aaron tugged down the edge of the harness and looked at the name tattooed at the base of Christelle's spine, at the very top of her rear furrow.

"See, Darling? I lied," she whimpered. "I did get you a present."

"It's lovely," he said. "The best I could have hoped for."

Then he took firm hold of Christelle's hips and pulled her onto his cock again, the single thrust taking her down to the very base. Christelle gasped. The quick insertion drove her over the edge, and she came as Aaron began to force her up and down on his cock. Her orgasm intensified as she tightened her thighs and pounded herself up and down on him, making the silver chain of the nipple clamps sway back and forth against her chest. The orgasm was unexpected in its intensity, and Christelle was still coming when Aaron groaned and let go inside her a moment later, filling her rear entrance with his come.

She relaxed against him, leaning back as his hands came up to pluck the clamps from her breasts. The sudden rush of sensation made her whimper in mingled pain and pleasure. "Did you like your present?" she asked.

He rolled her onto her belly across his knee. Tugging the strap of the harness down again, he ran his finger over the cursive letters of his name.

"It's a very merry Christmas," he said, and pulled her back onto him.

Slumber Party
by Nora McGaraghan

We thought we were being cute, having a slumber party, having a seance. There were six of us in my living room, all grown women wearing nightgowns and pajamas, playing games we hadn't played since puberty.

Jana was in the center of our circle, on her back. The rest of us had our fingers beneath her, ready to lift her when the time came. Tanya sat at the head of the circle, telling of the horrible way Jana had been murdered. At the end of her tale, we whispered together, "Light as a feather, stiff as a board," and lifted up on the count of three. It worked at first, we had her fairly high in the air before she started giggling. That made Sasha laugh, too, and the rest of us followed immediately, nearly dropping Jana onto my carpet. What happened next is inexplicable still. We went from laughing, rolling on the floor, to rolling with each other... kissing, snuggling, cuddling. I'd never done that with a girl before, *any* girl, and there I was making out with my best friends, first Eleanor, then Kathy, then Sasha, then Jana (the dead one).

We took turns, tussling, rocking together, helping each other out of our nightclothes until we were all naked. Tanya got the bright idea of lighting candles, and they cast a warm glow on our naked bodies. The different shades of skin excited me even more than I had been. My dark, cinnamon tone against Eleanor's pale, freckled body. Sasha's warm ebony arms on Jana's tan back. We were pretty together, the different shades, the different hair colors, the different sensations of lips I'd seen thousands of times but never kissed.

Without much shifting, we ended up in a circle again, this time, head to tail, mouth to mouth. I'd been kissing Eleanor, but then turned my head and found my lips pressed to Jana's shaven pussy. It surprised me how easy it was to make the transition, from mouth kissing to cunt kissing. It surprised me even more how much I enjoyed it, rolling onto my stomach to concentrate, to give Jana exactly what I like. I parted her nether lips and made a circle with my mouth around her clit. I sucked on it, teased it, then released and used my tongue as a probe inside her vagina.

She moaned aloud as I worked her, and I decided to get my hands in the action, fucking her with my middle finger and pointer together. I was so overwhelmed by the feeling of power that I didn't notice Eleanor moving behind me, getting on her stomach and parting the cheeks of my ass. Didn't notice until I felt her mouth there, her tongue lapping up and down before gently pressing inside me. I moved away from her, suddenly embarrassed, but she grabbed hold of my hips and pulled me back, whispering, "It's okay. It's all right. Let me...."

In that moment, I heard other voices, the sounds of my friends murmuring to each other. I looked around the room, struck again by the beauty of it, the wonder of it, all of us entwined with each other, lapping and overlapping each other's bodies. It was heavenly, transcendent, and I lost myself in it.

"More..."

Until I heard Jana begging me to make her come, requesting that I put my whole hand on her, in her, telling me how she wanted it. How she needed it.

And I returned to my job, aware of Tanya at my side, her mouth on Sasha and Sasha's mouth on her, and Kathy parting Sasha's asscheeks and helping out, going between Sasha and Eleanor. We worked together, as friends should, building the heat in the room until it hit a feverish pitch. Moaning, murmuring, coming. All of us together, all of us as one.

Cheating Time
by Jay Hall

I knew that Sheryl cheated on me, but I thought I could forgive her and forget about it. She seemed so contrite, tearfully admitting what had happened and begging for my forgiveness. For some reason, I thought I was a bigger person than I turned out to be. I didn't mean to get even—the fact is that I didn't know I was considering it. But I guess Sheryl knew. I guess she knew me better than I knew myself.

Lauren and I were assigned to work together on a project, a monster ad campaign our company had recently landed. It was mandatory for us to spend a huge amount of time together. Working, you know. Late nights. Early mornings. A few overnighters. A few weekends. We ended up crashing at the office every once in awhile, knowing we'd have to get up and work in a few hours anyway. It was only meant to be a time-saver.

But one of the mornings when I woke up on my leather sofa in the office, I found Lauren curled in my arms, and I knew it was going to happen. I guess I could have stopped it then. That's what an outsider might say. But an outsider simply can't see the situation from my perspective: her chestnut brown hair spread over me. Her peaceful, lovely face, relaxed in sleep. I pulled her closer and shut my eyes, joining her in the world of dreamland, deciding then and there that we would make love... and soon.

What I didn't expect was *how* soon.

Or how soon we'd be caught.

Sheryl must have sensed it in my behavior before I did. Maybe her own guilty conscience acted as a beacon to recognize mine. Christ, she'd fucked my best friend. She had a guilty enough conscience for both of us, didn't she? Turns out, she hired a private eye immediately, a man so good at his job that he caught us on film the very first time: Lauren splayed out on my drawing table, her pretty pussy held open by my slippery fingers, her nipples pinched between clothespins I'd snagged from the photo developing room. I'd tied her wrists with her own crimson hair ribbons, turning her into a present I couldn't wait to unwrap. She was beautiful bound up, exactly as I'd fantasized. Exactly as I'd known she'd be. Willing, humble, subservient. I paddled her ass with a wooden ruler I'd had in my top desk drawer for ages, punished the backs of her thighs with a thin, cardboard tube from the mailing room that made a delicious smacking sound when it connected with her naked skin.

The pictures came out well. I'm sure Sheryl got drippingly wet looking at them before ultimately confronting me with the evidence of my sins. The photos were black-and-white glossies of Lauren's face contorted in blissful ecstacy. Pictures of her striped ass, her parted thighs marked with the legal lines of my ruler. The images of me were all in motion, my hand pulled back to spank that gorgeous ass, my hips rotating as I thrust my cock into her willing mouth.

Those pictures are framed, now, and hanging in the private walk-in closet of our bedroom. Lauren's bedroom and mine. Turns out, I don't feel nearly as bad about cheating as I thought I would. In fact, I feel satisfied.

I only hope Sheryl has her own copies to look at during her long, lonely nights.

And I hope they make her happy.

Go!
By Ayre Riley

When he says to meet him in his upstairs home office, I know what's coming... I mean, I know what is going to happen. He has his leather chair pulled out in front of the mirror, and two ice-blue bottles of lube are lined up on the floor. There is a neatly folded crimson towel at the ready by the side of the chair.

He doesn't say anything at all. He simply strips and takes his seat. I perch on his lap, facing the mirror, without impaling myself on his cock. I feel how hard it is, and I sense that it's growing bigger by the second.

In the mirror, I watch as he spreads my legs wide, so that my knees are over the arm rests. Then he starts to play with my pussy. He opens me up, and I watch myself becoming aroused. More aroused every second. My pussy gets so pink and wet as his fingers play up and over my clit.

"Look at that," he says, "look how ready you are."

But he doesn't rush. The plan—always, the plan—is to let me come before he starts to fuck my ass. That way, I'm completely relaxed, my whole body overcome by bliss, and I can actually enjoy the sensation of being taken back there. Aside from that, there's always the happy chance that I'll come a second time. A chance that I particularly like to take. He goes slowly with his fingers, tracing around my clit, then up and over it. I don't watch my face while he works me. That feels too personal, somehow. Too confrontational. Instead, I watch only his fingers and my pussy, as if I'm staring at a private porn show put on just for me, by me.

Usually, I come, hard and sweet after several minutes of finger-fucking, and then he lubes himself up and glides in. I grip the arm rests to steel myself for the ride. He's hot by then, and he pumps me hard until he comes inside me. But today, something different happens. Today, as my clit grows more engorged and my appetite for lust increases, I whisper, "I want something new—"

"What?" His voice is a husky whisper.

"Don't make me come first—"

"What do you want?" he asks next, and the way he says it turns me on even more. As if he'll give me anything I say, anything I could possibly think of.

"Fuck me as I'm coming," I tell him. "Put it in me as I'm coming. Put your cock in my ass when I'm coming." The words are blurred and spilling quickly from my lips because I'm closer now. He sighs hard, and grows harder, pours lube down my slit and over his rod, and his fingers start to work with more finesse, knowing just what I like, until I can take nothing else. I'm right there, on the brink, and I say, "Go!"

And he's in me. Lubed and slick, right up in me. My hands grip the armrests as always, but this time, I'm coming as he fucks my asshole. Coming right up there with him, and my body milks him back, contracts on him, to make him come. Then we're both just left with the aftershocks, rocking in the chair, and staring at ourselves in the mirror.

We've always had a routine. It's always been the same. Up until now.

But in the future, when I say, "Go!" he'll know just what I mean—

#1 Fan
by Gabriella Wise

The sign said, "NO Admittance," but I pushed through it anyway. I'd been waiting for weeks, watching the employees of Astral Athena Records enter and exit, and I knew that the door wasn't guarded. I'd never done anything like this before, but I was desperate for a glimpse of my idol. I'd done my research. She was going to be recording in the studio for one day only. This was my chance.

I had on black satin pants, a long-sleeved black T-shirt, a bright yellow mail sack, and a black baseball cap emblazoned with the Astral Athena logo. I looked like all of the workers at Athena, young, hip, attractive. I slouched into the offices and nodded at the lovely woman seated at the reception desk, before heading past her to the mail room. She didn't stop me.

I knew the layout of the building, information I'd bribed from a friend who'd done temp work for the label. I made my way through the mail room to the back corridor, ducked into the first elevator, and cruised to the fifth floor, where the recording studios were.

Another receptionist guarded this area, but I slid by her with a priority envelope I pulled from my sack. "I need a signature from Ms. X," I told her. She looked me over, then waved me through. I took one step beyond the chrome doors and nearly bumped into my idol. I stopped, mumbled an apology, and lowered my head, waiting for her tirade. I'd heard about her awesome temper.

She surprised me. She lifted my chin with two fingers and stared into my eyes. I blushed, but held steady. "Excuse me," I said again. "I wasn't looking."

"I've seen you," she said. "But you don't work here."

I shook my head. There were others around us, and I sensed the largeness of the security guards, already nearby, waiting to drag me away.

"No, ma'am," I said softly. "But you might have seen me outside. I've been watching you."

She grinned, her exquisite smile lighting the severe features of her face. "That's right. And you've been at my concerts, too, haven't you?"

"Front row, center," I said, feeling those guards squeeze tighter to me, their muscles bulging.

My idol brushed them away and herded me into one of the offices, alone. Alone with *her*. She said, "You caught my eye. You're striking," and then moved back a step to stare at me before surprising me again. This time, she picked up a pair of scissors from the desk and quickly cut me out of my clothes. She remained dressed, in something soft and black. I liked the feel of her clothes against my naked skin. She seemed to like it, too. She caressed my back, the nape of my neck, kissed my eyebrows, my eyelashes, my cheekbones. She said, "It takes a lot to catch my attention. You've gone to some trouble."

I didn't answer. I couldn't. I responded to her kisses, opening my lips on hers, sliding my mouth to her neck, kissing her there, kissing her breasts through the gauzy dress, going on my knees to pleasure her, but she pushed me away. Now, I was on the floor, on my back. She straddled me, with her back to my face, and then went down into a sixty-nine, pressing her million-dollar lips to my naked pussy lips, diving inside my cunt with her warm tongue. She used her fingers as well as her mouth, running her hands on the insides of my thighs, tickling me, pinching my skin, pressing my thighs apart until I ached at the split of my body.

I couldn't totally believe what was happening to me. I'd woken often from this same dream before, from this fantasy, and I reached out and touched her with both hands to make sure she really was there.

"Is this real?" I asked, praying she wouldn't dissolve into air, into a mirage.

She lifted her mouth off me when she felt me touching her. She said, "Yes, it's real. I'm right here... can't you feel this?"

And then she put her mouth back where it had been, running

her tongue firmly along the opening of my pussylips, coaxing my clit until it stood out from its hood, huge and demanding, desperate to come. She was cruel to it, biting it, kissing it a little too hard, or, maybe just hard enough. And then, when I thought I really would die if this were a dream, she began murmuring to me as she worked, singing something soft and low into my pussy. Her song brought me to climax. I came to the rumbling vibrations of a voice I had come to over a stereo-headset countless times before.

I shuddered and grabbed her to me, wanting to reciprocate, but she easily freed herself from my embrace and stood, looking down at me. "It takes a lot to catch my attention," she said again, as if confused by her own actions.

I shrugged and sat up, wrapping my arms around myself, hiding, lowering my lashes, as always. Humble. But then, because it had to be said, I spoke. "Of course," I said, "I'm your number one fan."

Price to Pay
by Eric Reiter

When I want something, I get it. If I can't buy it, I'll steal it. If I can't find it, I'll have it made for me. I was born rich and I have turned my birthright into a fortune that would have impressed my father, a man not easily impressed by anything.

When I saw Elaine up on that stage at The Pussycat, holding onto the metal pole and swinging her slender body around it, I wanted her. She has that kind of a body that takes hours of toning daily, corded thighs, a flat, taut stomach, an ass you could cup in your hands. Her face was smooth and impassive, her eyes a dark, unwavering blue. I could tell she was wearing a wig, no one's has hair that highly glossed except Barbie, and I wanted to know what her real hair color was.

I requested a lap dance, paid for it, requested another, paid for that, and then asked her out.

She said, "I don't date the clientele."

I said, "You ought to just say 'yes' now and save yourself the trouble." She looked at me, questioning me with her cobalt eyes. "I always get what I want," I informed her, matter-of-factly.

She smiled at me, if you could call it that. Her eyes were unresponsive, the smile in her lips alone. She said, "You must have a nice life." One long beat. "I'm not for sale."

"Everyone has a price," I said, confidently. "Everyone."

She tilted her head, her eyes never wavering from mine. "You can't afford me," she said, next, then stood and walked to the backstage door.

I was there at opening the next night. And the next. She would give me lap dances, would tease me with her body, with her eyes that never changed. I bought her gifts, sapphire earrings, an emerald bracelet, and finally a thin black collar with diamond studs. That caught her eye and I smiled to myself, realizing I'd overplayed my hand. Realizing that the answer was so easy I hadn't even caught on. I walked to the back room, where the strippers change between shows, pushing past the bouncer who half-heartedly told me I wasn't allowed. $100 makes the talk inside, to paraphrase Tom Waits, and I handed over a bill and stalked after Elaine.

She was seated in front of a mirror, her hair up, her real hair, a finely spun golden mane, and she had the collar in her hands, fingering it. I met her eyes in the mirror, took the collar from her, and fastened it around her neck. Then, without speaking, I lifted her into my arms and carried her out the back way, to the parking lot. I had my convertible with me, and I set her in the back seat and peeled off her clothes, devouring her nipples, her flat stomach, her cunt. I had been restrained longer than I like, and I let her know it, ravaging her body with my tongue, fingers, fist. She moaned, grabbed my hair, let loose with a stream of foul language that made me even hotter. "Fuck me, oh, please, fuck me. With your hand... harder! Harder!"

"Whore," I spat, liking the way her eyes grew darker when I said it. At least I'd made them change. "You'll be mine. You said you didn't have a price. I didn't realize that meant I could take you for free." I slipped two fingers under her collar and tugged, so she could feel the bite of it. Then I went back down to her pussy and let her feel my bite there, on her cunt lips, on her clit, digging at her, lapping at her. It was so easy, making her feel it, breaking open that iced exterior and bringing her molten core to the surface. I swam in her, dined on her, ruined her for another.

Then I wrapped her in my coat, brought her into the front seat, and drove her home, telling her, along the way, of my plans. "You'll wear silk," I told her, "or satin, or leather, or vinyl. Or nothing. You'll have jewels and bathe in champagne, and anything you ask for will be yours." She turned her head on the seat and looked at me. "But you'll be mine," I said. "Mine," repeating the word and watching the way her eyes seemed to get softer, more willing. "And you'll do what I say."

"Yes, Sir," she murmured, agreeing, "whatever you say."

I grinned, thinking about what I wanted, what I desired. "Part your legs," I told her, "make yourself come while we drive." She set her feet on the dash, spread her thighs, and placed her fingers against her clit, rubbing at it while the cool night air washed over her body. She closed her eyes and rocked her hips against the leather seat.

I tried to keep my eyes on the road, but I stole silent glances, memorizing the look of ecstacy on her face, promising myself I would bring it to her often.

And forever.

Make It a Double
by Thomas S. Roche

My eyes roved wildly over the apartment as I paced back and forth.

"That definitely wasn't decaf," I said.

"You don't say," Sherry yawned. She had stripped down to her sleeping clothes: a white tank top and soft cotton shorts. She was curled up with a woolen blanket covering her legs and Sushi, our tabby cat, delicately washed his paws in her lap.

"I told them three times," I growled. "Decaf! Decaf! Decaf!"

"Maybe they couldn't hear you. You should have said it a fourth time."

Sushi regarded me with even less interest than my girlfriend. Sherry flicked the remote control from channel to channel as I walked a six-foot ellipse around the living room.

"I'm just about ready for bed," she told me.

"Not me," I snapped, and continued my pacing while she channel surfed.

"I think I'd better go to the gym," I finally said.

"They close at ten on Sundays," she told me.

"Damn it!"

Sherry looked at me with a faint smile on her lips. "You're sure that wasn't decaf?"

"Very funny."

She turned off the TV. "Come over here," she said, patting the sofa next to her. Sushi issued a fervent hiss and meowed discontentedly, then ran for the hills, darting across the living room toward the cat tree.

I looked at Sherry with mixed suspicion and paranoia. "Why?" I asked.

"I'm going to hit you over the head with a flower vase and knock you cold," she said.

"Please," I said, sitting next to Sherry on the sofa.

She was on me in an instant, bearing me back onto the sofa, crawling on top of me. She kissed me, her tongue sliding against mine as she reached her hands down my sweat pants.

"I know what'll calm you down," she said.

"I doubt it," I told her bitterly.

"But it certainly can't hurt," she said, pulling my sweats down. "Besides, your lips say *no* but your caffeinated cock says *make it a double*."

She took my cock in her hand as it hardened, then bent forward and wrapped her lips around it. I sighed softly as her mouth began to slide up and down on my shaft. I was painfully hard in an instant, and as Sherry's tongue swirled around my balls she stroked the tip of my cock with her thumb, caressing me in exactly the way she knows will make me come faster than fast. Her mouth worked around my head, her lips closed tight around it, and when she pulled back she moaned, her breath warm on my glistening prick.

"Come on," she cooed. "Let it all out. All that naughty caffeine into your cock. I want you to come French Roast, baby. Come on, I can take it."

Then her mouth was on my cock again, and my fingers were tangled in her hair as her head bobbed up and down. Long, low moans escaped my lips and I heard Sherry whimpering softly in the base of her throat. Her lips worked the head while her tongue lapped at the underside. Her hand began to pump the base.

Sushi was sitting at the top of the cat tree blinking in bemusement. He made eye contact with me and pawed the air. I would have sworn the little bugger was shooting me the feline version of a high-five.

Sherry's mouth rose off of me for just an instant. "Come on," she said. "Let it all out." Her mouth came down over my cock again and she hungrily pumped it, sucking me harder than before.

I moaned, my hips lifting, and let go. Pleasure washed over me as I came in Sherry's mouth, listening to her tiny whimpers as she swallowed and hungrily sucked for more. A big sigh came out of me as I finished shooting.

Sherry snuggled up on top of me, cuddling close. She whispered softly in my ear.

"You're right," she said, licking her lips. "It definitely wasn't decaf."

I smiled ruefully.

"So now *you'll* be up all night?" I said.

She giggled and kissed me on the neck.

"Yeah," she told me, her fingers spidering up my stomach underneath my sweatshirt to tease my nipple. "But it's not a problem, baby. Not a problem at *all*."

Sushi jumped on top of us and began to knead Sherry's hip.

Desert Flower
by Glenda Woodams

The drive to Vegas from Los Angeles is out-of-control boring. Nothing to see. Nothing to do. Nothing to look forward to except the next fast food meal. It's always been that way for me in the past. But then, I'd never traveled with Tania before.

She's a photographer for some of the most avant-garde fashion magazines in the industry. We met on a shoot in Hollywood, and she invited me to accompany her to Vegas. I was impressed by her candor, and by her convertible Jag, and I said yes. But sprawling my long legs on the dashboard, considering the five long hours to kill, I had sudden reservations.

As soon as we were out of the city and had hit the desert, however, Tania began to change. She'd been quiet the first forty-five minutes of the drive. Now she started talking, telling me how much she liked the desert, the air, the hot sand, the way the heat looked when she photographed it.

"How do you shoot heat?" I asked.

She didn't respond for a few minutes, and just when I thought she wasn't going to answer my question, she pulled the car over. I looked at her, questioning her, and she said, "Come on," grabbed her camera, hopped out of the car, and made her way into the sand. I followed. What else could I do?

When we reached a group of boulders, hot from the sun, she said, "Strip."

"Here?"

She nodded.

I shrugged—this was more exciting than driving—and pulled off my T-shirt, boots, and jeans. She had her camera poised at me before I was completely naked. Then, with only a little direction from her, I began to pose. I could feel the sun baking my naked skin, could feel the blue of the sky caressing me in a way I never had. And as I turned, as I showed off, I tried to see what she described, the heat... but I couldn't.

When she set her camera on a rock, I knew what was coming. She had that look, the look she'd worn when I met her at the shoot, and she came forward, teeth bared, eyes hard and silent. Her hands on me were insistent, probing, squeezing my small breasts, running the length of my body, parting my cunt lips and revealing me. She went on her knees in the sand, using her thumbs and pointers to pinch open my nether lips, to probe at me until my come was dripping into the sand below.

She said, "Piss for me."

I looked at her, startled, but saw that hard thing in her eyes that told me not to argue. I squatted and she put her hand out and let the warm stream stain her fingers before it landed in the sand. She caught the last few drops with her tongue before turning me around and bending me over, standing and freeing her synthetic cock, plunging it into me.

There were other cars driving by, and they slowed to watch these two animals rutting against each other. She fucked me hard, driving me forward until I pressed my hands flat in the sand, open and offering her all.

Tania said, "I wish someone could take our picture like this." Her words were low. "Raw against the rock and sand and sky."

I couldn't answer. Felt her filling my insides with that huge cock, felt my muscles grabbing onto it like a life preserver and trying to keep it in me.

"We'll set up the tripod on the way back," she said, still going at it. I was stunned at how she could talk while she fucked. "We'll capture it all on film. You and me. You pissing into the sand. That was fucking gorgeous, you know it?" Slamming me to the hilt, now, not even breathing hard as she did it. "Your golden stream of piss against the golden sand."

I couldn't answer, just kept myself bent and thought about what she had said earlier, in the car. The desert is magical. Life grows out of nothing. And the heat, the heat that you can actually see surrounds you. I blinked and opened my eyes and I saw the shimmering light before me, saw the silver and gold halos of air all around me. White and glistening, all around me.

Saw the heat.

New Tricks
by Nica Jacobs

My new dog was a biter. Not just a chewer, ingesting my shoes, my sofa, my brand-new prize Chanel purse, but people, as well. And, although Chanel is more important to me than most people I know, it took Rex biting my beloved sister for me to finally enroll him in obedience training school.

"Get rid of him," Sheila suggested instead. She wasn't pleased with the tiny little teeth marks on her delicate ankle.

"No," I told her. I had rescued him from the pound. I wasn't about to return him. He wasn't a bad dog, simply an untrained one.

"You can't teach an old dog new tricks," my sister offered unhelpfully. I ignored her.

I'm the type of person who likes to drop off my laundry and pick it up clean. I don't do dishes; I have a dishwasher. I don't make my bed; I have a maid. When I found out I had to enroll in the school, myself, I was a little peeved.

"Can't you just train him, and let me pay you?" I asked.

The dark-haired owner of the school shook his head. "You need to be able to give Rex commands. He will learn to obey you, but you must be present for his training."

I heaved a huge sigh, but then remembered my sister's angry look. "Okay, fine," I said, perhaps not using my most polite or accommodating tone. "Whatever."

I decided to take private lessons, which cost more but would be over sooner. It wasn't as bad as I'd thought. The trainer, Johnny, was stunning, a tall, dominating man with a deep voice. When the lessons were finally over, Rex was a different dog. As I settled up, Johnny took Rex's leash from me and set my dog free in the play area to roam.

"What's going on?" I asked, signing my check.

Without speaking, Johnny took me by the hand and led me

into his office. He closed and locked the door and said, "You're rather spoiled, aren't you?"

I looked at him, shocked. Was this how he talked to all of his clients? Up until now, he'd been incredibly professional. While I stood there, mouth open, he continued, "You're used to getting your own way. Always. It's obvious from the way you behave—or misbehave."

I started to reply, angrily, and was stunned as he began to undo his leather belt and slip it free from the loops. "You're the one in need of training," he said, motioning for me to come closer. I hesitated, looking at his long legs, his strong body, the firm set of his lips as he waited. Then I walked to his side and said, in my most humble voice, "Maybe...."

He didn't let me finish. He bent me over his desk, yanked down my slacks, and, doubling his belt, gave me a hiding. I hadn't been punished like that in a long, long time. Not since I'd broken up with my last beau... the one I was replacing with Rex. My ass stung with each blow and I whimpered, like a puppy, and squirmed. But I didn't try to get away.

Johnny said, "You don't know how to treat your superiors, do you? You just pout and whine and demand things. You need a long, healthy training session." Whipping me as he spoke, demanding I answer his questions with, "Yes, Sir. Whatever you say, Sir."

Finally, he was done, and he pushed me onto my hands and knees and said, "Look at you. Groveling. Now, do you agree with me? Do you need some training?"

I nodded, "Yes, Sir."

"Good girl. We'll start tonight." He wrote down his address and handed it to me. "Don't be late."

I shook my head. "No, Sir I won't be late." My heart was leaping in my chest. I'd finally found a man who understood me. What I wanted. Needed. Craved.

As I got ready to leave, adjusting my clothes, fixing my hair, Johnny came toward me with a thin, leather collar. He lifted my hair and placed the thing around my neck, quickly buckling it.

"Now," he said, "Be a good girl until tonight, and I'll let you keep that."

Ducking my head, lowering my eyes, I said, "Yes, Sir. I promise." Then I went to collect Rex and together we left the obedience school.

In the car, on the drive home, I looked at Rex. He was panting, almost grinning, happy to be in the car. I stroked his dark red fur and ran my fingers over his leather collar. Then I turned the rear-view mirror a little to look at my own leather collar. My smile was as wide as his as I said aloud, to myself, "Maybe, just maybe you *can* teach an old dog new tricks."

Vocational Hazard
by Sage Vivant

At six-feet-one-inch tall and 200 pounds, Karl was not a likely burglar. He couldn't easily slip into unforgiving spaces or pass unseen behind parked cars. Nevertheless, he'd had modest success in his career, breaking and entering undetected into some of the neighborhood's better homes.

He'd been watching this particular house for about a month and knew that only the housekeeper was in residence—the owners were on some extended vacation. He never killed people who got in his way, but the housekeeper would certainly meet with unfortunate consequences if she decided to protect the place she was hired to clean.

The window slid up smoothly, and he crawled into the bedroom with practiced stealth. Once both his feet were on the carpeted floor, he heard bed sheets rustling and jerked his head around to follow the sound. Illuminated by the stream of moonlight from the window, the housekeeper sat upright in her bed, her knees trembling at her chin.

This would normally be the point at which he'd physically restrain the person who posed a threat to his mission. Instead, he stood immobile, locked in a gaze with those enormous green eyes. Though she watched him expectantly, there were equal parts fear and invitation in her expression.

"Maybe you should tie me up," she whispered.

He always had rope with him. As he moved to pull it from his pocket, she spoke again.

"I have some rope in the nightstand."

His cock thought first. It told him to command her to strip. She obeyed. Never taking her big, round eyes off him, she spread out her alabaster body like a willing participant. Her breasts were small and her pussy hairless.

He withdrew his own rope and tied her wrists to the

formidable bedposts. When he spread her legs to secure her ankles, the deep fragrance of her cunt's readiness made him stop. She was still staring at him when he bit the fabric of his glove to pull it off his hand. He immediately touched his uncovered hand to her steamy wet snatch. With no hair to catch her moisture, her juices coated his hand almost instantly.

The efficiency expert in him decided time was at a premium. He threw her legs over her head and unzipped his fly. Out came his thick, steely cock, which now became the focus of the housekeeper's gaze—until he rammed it into her. The housekeeper's soft whimpers made him harder, made him want to fuck her more furiously.

Her beautiful eyes finally closed. His thrusts had pushed her up toward the headboard and her head now tapped it every time he pushed. He didn't want to come yet, he decided.

Untying her wrists, he maneuvered her onto all fours so that her perfect little white ass stuck up in the air, asking to be taken. He positioned himself behind her and pumped, breathlessly watching her ass cheeks reverberate as he fucked her. He heard her panting and felt her asshole grip him before it spasmed into an orgasm.

As his hot juices spewed into her, he made a mental note to come back the following night... to rob the house.

First-Class Service

by Edward Van Houten

I was flying Concierge Class on a red-eye to Paris for business. To my relief, I had most of the cabin to myself, aside from a heavy-set man who had fallen asleep even before take-off. I envy people who have that sort of ability to relax. I'm not one who can sleep on planes. But as it was, on this plane, there was someone special to capture my attention: our flight attendant. She was a pixie-blonde with an attitude. Her name tag read, "Oh, Miss!"

I liked her. I liked her a lot.

As the flight got underway, "Oh Miss" swished her hips up and down the aisle, acting as if the cabin were full when I tried to talk with her. "Just a minute," she said, "I'll be with you presently."

But as the flight continued, she began to talk with me. There wasn't much else for her to do with her passenger list at two instead of twelve, and one of the two completely comatose. She perched on the arm of the chair across the aisle from mine, and absentmindedly twirled a strand of her hair around her finger as she spoke.

"Will you have time to sightsee?"

I didn't catch her question, was too busy sneaking a peek at her long legs in that short skirt, shorter still now that she was sitting. Sightsee? I *already* was. I saw London, I saw France.... She continued, oblivious, listing the various "hot" places to visit until she caught my glazed look. It startled her. She dropped her hand from her hair to her throat. Her pale skin was so white there, almost translucent, and I could see the veins just under the surface. I leaned across the aisle and replaced her fluttering fingertips with my own hand, feeling the beat of her heart, the pulse of it.

"Can I—" she started, squinting, losing her attitude suddenly, "I mean, do you need something else?" She half-rose as she said it, and I took the opportunity to stand, too, to glance quickly at our sleeping companion, to herd "Oh, Miss" into the lavatory and lock the door.

"I need something..." I said, forcefully, turning her so that her face was to the mirror and her ass was to me. "Yes, I need something." I lifted her skirt, yanked down her panties. She pressed back against me, and at the connection of her naked skin with my hard clothes-clad cock, she sighed with relief.

"Not to worry," I told her, "I've got what you need, too."

In a completely humble tone she asked, "Will you put it in me? Will you fuck me?"

I didn't answer her with words. Instead, I used my rod as my voice, sliding it between her thighs and going to work, moving it deep within the tight confines of her cunt. Her scent filled the small lavatory, that subtle tangy aroma of sex and wet and heat. Her thighs were dripping, lubricating my cock so that when I decided to put it in her ass, it was all wet and ready.

She kept her eyes locked on mine in the mirror. But her pale skin took on a healthy glow and she unbuttoned her uniform top to show me a beautiful set of breasts, captured in black lace.

I ran my fingers over her nipples, pinched them one at a time, in order with the rhythm I was fucking her. She took it in stride, bucking against me, as if she had her back door filled everyday. She knew how to go for a naughty, fucking ride.

As she began the steady rise to climax, there was a knock at the door, followed by the voice of the once-snoring passenger, "Oh, Miss! Excuse me!"

But my miss was too busy to answer with anything other than an "Ohhhhh" of her own.

Dressing Room
by Elle McCaul

I wandered through the Designer Clothing section, looking for a three-way mirror. When I found one, I realized another woman was checking out my reflection, her eyes focused on the curves of my ass. Always the exhibitionist, I turned around and around, admiring my slender thighs, the haughty curve of my bum, shown to perfection in the CK jeans.

But the woman was staring at me in a way that suggested she might be more than a casual admirer, staring for much longer than is polite. I walked over, finally, and asked, "Do I know you?"

She shook her head, blushing as dark as her sleek red hair, and said, "You've got the last pair of size two Calvins. The saleslady says they won't get any more in that style. I was wondering if you were going to buy them. Or, if not, if I could try them on."

I looked at myself in the mirror. I liked the way the jeans fit. Classy, body-hugging jeans are difficult to find.

"They look great on you," she said next, reading my mind, blushing even harder. "I'm not trying to influence your purchase. I was just waiting for your decision."

I wanted the jeans. But I started to want this woman, too. Which was more important? I shrugged and said, "I've got a million pairs of jeans at home. You can have them if they fit you."

Then I motioned for her to follow me to the dressing room. Gratefully, her green eyes shining at me, she did. It was obvious she was planning on waiting outside my dressing room, but, on a whim, I grabbed her hand and pulled her in with me.

Without giving her time to avert her eyes, I slid out of the jeans and kicked them over to her. "Try them on here," I said, "if they fit, we'll decide who looks better."

She swallowed hard, undid the buckle of her slacks and slid them off. Then, not meeting my eyes, she pulled on the CKs, still warm from my body. They looked divine on her. We both knew it.

She primped for a moment in front of the mirror, then shyly met my eyes.

"You'll owe me, you know," I said, taunting, wondering what her response would be.

She surprised me, went down on her knees on the dressing room carpet and pressed her face against my panty-clad pussy, kissing me along the seam, wetting me there with her tongue. She was like an animal, sweet and shy, yet totally natural, taking what she wanted, giving what I needed.

I moved her aside and pulled off my panties, then let her continue, watching in the mirrors as she lapped and licked at my dripping cunt. I was making a puddle of glistening nectar on the seat of the dressing room, but I didn't stop her. I let her bathe my clit, instructed her to use her fingers.

"Inside me," I said.

"Oh, yes..." her pointer and middle finger rocketed deep in my cunt, her tongue played magic tricks with my clit, tickling, teasing. I was close to coming, but I needed something more... something... The beyond-snotty saleslady knocked at the door, asking, "Is everything all right."

And, exhibitionist that I confessed to being, I moaned, "Yesss... oh, yesss..." as I hit the peak and crested downward. The saleslady left us alone after that. I looked down at my new, nameless friend, and grinned.

She stood and took off the jeans, sliding back into her own outfit.

"You know," she said, "they fit us both. Maybe we could share them. Split the cost, then take turns wearing them."

I looked at her for a moment. "When it's my turn, I guess I'll owe you," I said, and my brand-new friend nodded as she tossed me the jeans.

The Form and the Function
by Tyler Morgan

They were both watching me. Joe, who owns the gym, and who's been my best male buddy since freshman year in college, and this girl. This hot, young redheaded athletic chicklet riding the stationary bike on her journey to nowhere. She was wearing a turquoise leotard and slim gray sweatpants, and her corkscrew curly hair was pulled off her face with a lilac headband.

I hadn't seen her there before, but from the way she was staring at me—well, it looked as if she liked what *she* saw. The mirrored wall of the gym is intended for clients to watch themselves while they pump iron. It helps you make sure that each rep is smooth, fluid, that you don't lose your pace or your concentration. I know the drill. The rest of the world can fade away when you're in the middle of a good workout. But this evening, eyes were focused on parts of the body that didn't belong to the owner. Joe was watching her, and she was watching me, and I was watching both of them. In a game to glance when nobody could catch you, we were all both losing and winning.

There were only the three of us that night. Saturdays at 10 are generally slow. That's why I like to workout at off hours. This Saturday was the weekend before Christmas, and nobody was around. Nobody but us. But that was perfectly fine. The three of us made the perfect team, even if nobody was ready to admit it yet. Not with our voices, anyway.

Only with our eyes.

That girl was intense. That hot, hot girl. She was clocking me like a hungry feline. And, oh, did I ever want to feel her full, pretty lips devour me. So what did Joe have to do with this? Well....let me tell you about Joe.

He and I go way back, like I said. And although I know that he puts on a straight-act, he really doesn't care much about the sex of the people he sleeps with. As a fitness expert, he is all about the body. The form. The function. He competes in contests, the type intended for no-steroid-use athletes. He is pure within his body and within his mind. Or, at least, he is when it comes to working out. When the subject turns to fucking, he is as dirty as they come.

Or as he comes—

Or she comes—

My mind was a jumble of these sorts of thoughts, so much so that when the pretty jock girl made her way to my side, she caught me off guard.

"Hey—" she said. "Joe tells me you're good."

I couldn't answer at first. Good at what? Good at making some lithe little athlete such as herself have multiple orgasms on my tongue? Good at holding a lover down to my bed, my hands on her wrists, our bodies pumping together? Good at pushing a pretty minx up against the shower and going at her? Yes, I was very good at all those things. Tonight, I knew precisely how I'd like to start, pulling her Lycra leggings off and using them as bindings to capture her slender wrists to the rack at the far wall—

"Good at spotting," she said, indicating the free weights in the far corner.

"Oh, yeah," I told her. "Sure—"

I followed behind her, checking out her fine ass in those sleek-fitting slacks. And then I spotted for her as she pressed iron. She was impressive. A girl her size. She knew what she was doing. As did Joe, who came up behind me as the girl did her last rep, and said, "I've locked up."

We both turned to look at him, the girl, gazing at us from her upside-down viewpoint, me staring over my shoulder. "Nobody's around," he said next. And that was it. Not even an invitation. Just a statement. The girl squirmed around into a sitting position and gently raked her fingers along my chest. When she reached the bottom of my red cotton T-shirt, she started to pull it up. I immediately helped her, tossing the shirt in the corner and nodding for her to strip as well. Joe was ahead of both of us, out of his workout gear in seconds. He had a bottle of something in his hand, an oily product used for making athletes gleam in competition. When she was naked, Joe began to oil her up.

"He says you're good," she grinned over her shoulder at me. I stared only in the mirror, watching her skin take on a warm golden glow.

"Yeah," I said again. "I'm good—"

The three of us moved tight together on a cobalt blue mat in front of the mirrors. Joe in front of her, facing her, me in back. I could look over her shoulder and stare into my friend's gray-green eyes, or I could glance in the mirror and see the three of us moving together like a well-oiled machine, which really is what we were.

A fucking machine. One that might not make any of us stronger, but would definitely take us to the point of no-resistance, to a place where all of us desperately wanted to go.

I slid easily into her ass as Joe probed her in front. His fingers overlapped mine at her waist, and I had a flash of us in the past, bent over one of the weight benches, me behind him—him behind me—never has mattered much to us.

"It's all about form," Joe says. "Don't do it if you're not going to do it right."

So that's what we did. The three of us. Me in her and Joe in her, and the pretty toned girl pumping back and forth between her two rock-solid men. That's exactly what we did, following Joe's mantra—

We did everything right.

The Lizard Queen
by Julia Richards

I'm not a ghoul. I don't usually hang out in cemeteries. But on our trip to Paris, my lover insisted on visiting Jim Morrison's grave at the Pere LaChaise. "Can't we just say we went?" I asked, not excited about spending a day with the dead. "No one will know."

"What's your problem?" she demanded, shooting me a look. "It's only a cemetery."

We went, of course. We do whatever Laura says we're going to do. Always. As we made our way into the place, the gatekeeper told us that they were almost ready to close. "We'll be quick," Laura promised in French. I was glad for that. The days were shorter and a cool wind had begun to blow, stirring the leaves around us.

As we made our way through the graves, Laura grabbed me by the hand and pulled me toward one of the mausoleums. One that had a broken entrance. I shook my head and tried to stop her. But there really is no stopping Laura. When she says "jump," I bounce like a fucking bunny.

Inside the mausoleum, she crouched down, pulling me with her. "We'll wait until the keeper locks up for the night," she said, "and then we'll go find the Lizard King." I was against it, but we don't have a democracy. The last rays of sunlight hit the stained glass window, bathing us in shimmering blues and reds. The light fell on Laura's face, on her eyes, and they glowed, a green fire burning wickedly within them.

While we were waiting, we ended up kissing, and that's always good. I had my shirt off and my bra undone and Laura warmed my nipples with her mouth before clamping them with the ridged clips she always carries with her. The clips have a chain hanging between them, and the weight of it makes my pussy ache with want.

"Please," I said, pushing against her, begging with my body and with my words until she undid my jeans and prodded me with her fingers, pinching my clit until it felt like it would burst, treating me to a few soft caresses and lots of the pain that I crave. She knows how to make me come, but she didn't. She kept me on edge, fucking me, fucking *with* me, having me stand so that she could bite my shaved cunt lips until I was marked by her pointed teeth, nearly out of my skin from wanting to come so bad. She wouldn't let me, though. She never makes it easy for me.

It was dark by then, and we were cramped in the small quarters, so Laura pulled me out of the mausoleum after her, insisting I leave my top and jeans in a heap. I wandered naked behind her, feeling the cool bite of the fall air on my pale, smooth skin, nearly glowing beneath the moonlight. We finally found the grave, and Laura sat on the headstone and pulled out her switchblade.

"Come here," she ordered.

I did, going on my knees on top of the grave and waiting. She's into carving, now, scarification, and she drew a design on my back, over the silver lines of old scars and the dark purplish lines of new ones. I held my breath and felt the blood run free, dropping down onto the grave, and onto Jim's bones. The pain of it was good, clarifying, and I could feel the distant climax rise within me again, coming so close to it that I felt dizzy and disoriented.

I don't know when the music started, the haunting few bars of "The End." All I know is that Laura was there, with her knife and her attitude, and then she wasn't. And I was lying on Jim's grave watching him get into leather jeans and toss his hair out of his eyes.

"Pamela's going to love you," he said, reaching for my hand. I looked down, at the velvet dress that had woven itself over my skin, at the red roses that were growing where my drops of blood had fallen. Then I took his hand and followed him into the night.

Jake's Apartment
by Tasha Dillon

Jake's apartment is less than five miles from mine. I can make the trip in under three minutes if I catch all the lights. At two a.m., there are few cars to get in my way, and my fear of cops decreases in direct proportion to my desire to get laid. If I were a different sort of chick, I'd burn rubber in my haste to get to his place.

On this night, I find him up, as I thought he would be, wide awake and relaxing on his battered blue sofa, watching the type of late night black-and-white movie that isn't considered a classic. It's just considered old. I see through his large picture window that he's watching the flick with an intense expression of concentration on his strikingly handsome face, and he only casually turns to look at me when I slide my key in his door and turn the knob, then shut the door quietly behind me.

There's a moment when I actually think he's going to make me beg. That he's going to explain in a dark tone how interested he is in the plot of this fifty-year-old dog of a movie, that I'll have to wait until the film is over before we fuck. If he says that, I'm going to cry. I know it. I'm going to dissolve into some pathetic creature who will absolutely beg him to take me. No holds barred. I'll fall down on my knees in front of him, scrambling to undo the fly of his faded jeans, to withdraw his cock and suck it deep down my throat.

Don't make me beg, I think. *Just fuck me.*

Please, just fuck me.

I got so wet on the drive over that I'm almost out of my head with lust. Sure, the journey was brief, I know, but then I was actually wet before I left my apartment. Sopping as I slid into my lizard-green hot pants and my stretchy black off-the-shoulder top. So amazingly wet as I slicked on my favorite lipstick and fluffed my hair. I look as if I'm ready for a night out at one of our favorite clubs, when all I'm interested in is a night on the floor with Jake. Or on the sofa. On the balcony. Outside under the stars. Anywhere.

So don't make me beg, I think. *Come on, Jake. Don't make me.*

Then, like an angel, he smiles at me, mutes the TV, and stands. We don't go to his bedroom. Not tonight. There isn't time, and he knows it. Maybe he can smell the arousal on me. Maybe he's feeling as intensely turned-on as I am. Instead of ushering me to his bedroom, he brings me to a chair and sits me down, then pulls my stretchy black top down past my shoulders to reveal my naked breasts. Can't wear a bra with this sort of flimsy contraption. That's my excuse, anyway. He bends to kiss my tits, his mouth soft and warm on my nipples, and he moves back and forth, making sure to treat both equally.

I'm humming with pleasure already. And I close my eyes, feeling the movie flicker over my shut lids. Seeing without seeing.

Jake goes on his knees to kiss me, and I feel my lipstick smear from my mouth to his, feel his teeth on my bottom lip, tugging, worrying my lip for me. He nips and bites his way back down again to my breasts, and then he moves his hands to cradle my waist. I think that I'll have to stand to get my teensy shorts off, but he has other ideas. First, he slides his hands up my thighs, slipping under the edges of my shorts. Somehow he manages to touch my pussy through my panties but under my hot pants, and I feel myself shift forward on the seat, groaning at the connection.

Now, he moves his hands and rips open the side zip, then slides my shorts off and down. When he sees the pretty little G-string I have on underneath, *he's* the one to sigh. He presses his lips to the lacy hot-pink triangle covering my pussy. The fabric provides no protection at all from the warm soft wetness of his mouth. But that's okay. I don't want protection. I want the wetness. Drippy and hot. I want everything about this—the way he slides his tongue in dreamy designs over my pussy lips, traces invisible pictures around and around. He kisses and licks until I am babbling urgent requests for him to continue, to please not stop, to just make it happen. And he does.

He eats me relentlessly until I come on his tongue, and only *then* does he slide my G-string off and turn me so that I'm bent over the chair. He takes his position behind me, releasing his hard-on and fucking me deep and strong. I gaze at the floor as I feel a second climax build, and I memorize the patterns in the rug, intricate boxes within boxes in shades of brown and beige and gold. The designs remind me of his tongue against my clit, and I run one hand between my legs, touching myself when I sense Jake is about to come.

We climax together—in thundering waves—in the late night movie glow of Jake's apartment.

The Party
by Alison Tyler

Carrie put her hand on my arm as she made her way through the party. That light touch, almost a tickle, made me turn and watch her move through the crowd. And in that second, I wanted more.

Yes, we'd met several times in the past. We'd been at the same cook-outs, the same outdoor concerts, the same beach parties, each of us knowing different friends within the core group. But now, I wanted to learn more about her, and it was all because of that single whisper-soft touch. Trying not to look like a stalker, I followed her through the room. She sensed my presence, and my interest, immediately, looking over her shoulder at me. Winking and then nodding with her sweetly sharp chin upward.

I raised my eyebrows at her. What exactly did 'up' mean?

She parted her lips, and I saw the glint of metal of the piercing on her tongue. "Follow me," she mouthed silently. As it was what I was already doing, I simply continued, my eyes on her lithe body as I walked behind her up the stairs at the back of the house. Up to a series of empty bedrooms. We chose the first, undressing as soon as she shut and locked the door behind us, falling into the bed in our haste. Then we were on each other. Hands exploring. Tongues testing.

I'd like to say that we spent hours on the foreplay, but we didn't. We got down to serious business right away. After all, neither one of us knew when we'd be interrupted. Still, I took my time, teasing her, pleasing her, memorizing the curves and valleys of her body.

Carrie twisted her fingers through my long dark hair, stroking it, and she sighed and whispered nonsense words that sounded like music. My new lover liked what I was doing. I could tell. Encouraged, I pressed my lips against a pussy that had a musky scent of real life to it. Not the antiseptic flavor of an overly douched cunt. Not the floral nonsense you read about in romance novels.

Nobody smells like lavender. Nobody tastes like rose petals. People have real smells and flavors and that's what makes them sexy.

This lovely vixen had a scent that was tinted with the smell of body lotion, but tasted of honest warm skin beneath it. Her wetness lingered on my lips and on my tongue. I lapped at her, thrust my tongue deep inside her, felt the inner ridges of her body. But before I could get her off, she pushed me back on the bed and swiveled over me, positioning herself with her mouth over my sex and her pussy poised just before my lips. Again, I opened my mouth to taste her, but this time, as soon as my tongue connected with her skin, I felt her tongue probing me down below, echoing my actions.

The silver metal ball in the center of her tongue tapped against my clit. This sensation sent a surge of pleasure through me. Concentric circles started in my pussy and radiated out to the tips of my fingers and toes, like ripples in a lake moving outward toward shore. It was delicious, how she used the metal ball to start me up, following with the flat of her tongue like a tool to tickle my nether lips, to probe between them. I didn't stop making spirals with my own tongue, but I began to buck against my lover's mouth as she worked me.

Carrie knew what she was doing. She made the same circles with her tongue that I make with my fingers whenever I climax solo. Even better than what she was doing with her tongue was her steady monologue. While she worked me, she continued to murmur those nonsense words, saying, "my sweet girl," and "that's right, pretty thing," and "come on, baby."

Her voice sent vibrations swelling throughout my whole body, echoing and re-echoing. This was intense, hearing her voice as I felt it, and soon, I was coming, my inner muscles rapidly contracting, pulling in hard and fast. Knowingly, she slid two fingers up inside my cunt and let me squeeze and release them while I climaxed. I tightened on her fingers, spasms building and receding while my breathing caught in my chest, until I was leaning up in the bed, pulling her body harder against mine. She came a moment later, as if spurred on by my pleasure, and I felt the tremors silently wash through her until once again she was still.

I thought we'd take a break then. Roll languidly in the rumpled sheets. Trace our fingers over each other's bodies. Relax and remember how to breathe once again. She had other plans.

In the hazy darkness, she rolled me over, and then I felt her hands parting my rear cheeks, her lips meeting my peach-like split. Kissing me there. Licking me. I closed my eyes tight at the decadent sensation as she spread my heart-shaped cheeks even wider apart, stretching me open. Air touched the wet places she'd kissed, and I shivered. Each move she made back there sent new waves of pleasure through my pussy. And then I felt that metal ball come into play as her tongue thrust into my asshole.

The silvery ball stroked me inside as her tongue went in deep. I moaned out loud, couldn't help it, and brought one hand down beneath my body, stroking my clit as she continued to tongue-fuck my ass. Nothing had ever felt that extreme. My pussy pulsed and twitched, my heart raced, and soon, too soon, I was coming again. Shaking the bed. My lover held onto my waist with her hands, keeping me steady as she licked my hole through the orgasm.

Extending it. Stretching it. Taking me to places I hadn't known existed outside of fantasies, and making them real.

Without Her
by Jay Hall

I never would have planned it to happen the way it did. I mean, you hear people say stuff like that all the time, and you shrug to yourself, "If you didn't want it to happen, then you could have stopped it." But now I'm on the other side of things, and I see life from a new perspective—and I'm starting to understand.

I take pictures of cheating couples for a living. That's what I do. I'm a private eye. Give people the evidence they need to confirm suspicions they already have. It never works the other way. By the time people come to me for my services, they already have the details. They just don't want to face the facts. In plain English, I never prove innocence; I only confirm guilt.

I guess I'd have to say I always felt above it all. Knowing I'd never bend that low, cheat on someone I loved, make them feel the kind of pain I'd seen so many times in a woman's eyes. Why would I do that? I'd simply break off the relationship, sever the ties, and then plunge the filly that needed plunging.

Innocent thoughts of a neophyte. I never will be that innocent again.

Julianne and I had been together for eight months, a record for me. I'm a bit of a slut, you may have guessed that from my attitude. I don't like to be held in. I don't cheat—or I *didn't* cheat—but my relationships rarely have lasted longer than a month. But Julie was special, pretty and smart and giving. She had me ensconced in her apartment by our third date. (I never told her I kept my own place, paying rent on an empty room as a back-up in case things didn't work out.)

I was on a job, snapping pictures of a couple from an office building across the way. I had my telephoto lens, had everything I needed. But, as I clicked each shot, as I stared at the lovers entwined, I felt something new. A desire I'd never felt before. The two lovers were both attractive, but the sub was something special, something worthwhile. She had a mane of dark hair and a face like an angel. I wanted her. I needed her.

I approached her with the pictures, something I'd never done before. "Your boyfriend hired me," I said, "I don't have to give him these... but I will."

She looked at me with angelic blue eyes and she swallowed hard and invited me into her office. She took the pictures from me and placed them in her top dresser drawer. Then she stared at me, begging with her eyes and then her mouth, "Please..." (just what I wanted to hear), "I'll do anything."

She sucked my cock, she offered me her ass, she called me Daddy, let me do things to her. Anything I wanted to. I tied her up. Took pictures of her with my cock in her ass and a dildo in her cunt, and a third, massive toy in her mouth. She looked glamorous when she was wallowing in the filth. But there was something even more than that. Other girls will let you do stuff to them. And if you can't find the right ones for free, you can always pay. But this girl was magical. There was something about her, something transcendent. Her smell, her face, the way she batted her eyes.

The way she said, "I love you, oh, how I love you."

I can't describe that. Can't believe I fell for it.

I defiled her. I had her all chained up and suspended from the ceiling. I had her any way I wanted her. Fulfilled every fucking fantasy I'd ever even thought about. Every image that had ever flickered through my twisted mind.

And when she went to Julianne and told her all, I can't describe that either. But I sit here alone in this empty room and I wait for the phone to ring, wait for her to call. And I wonder what it was I saw through that telephoto lens of mine. Something angelic? Something of the devil? I don't know.

I only hope she'll call.

Summer Rain
by Thomas S. Roche

"Look at that rainbow," Lindsay said. "It's incredible."

It had been raining earlier as we drove through the Napa Valley, a warm summer rain that turned the wine-swollen countryside to great fields of mud. About a half-hour before, the rain had trailed off, and now hanging in an arch over the hills was a rainbow so brilliant it hurt my eyes to look at.

"We've got to take a picture," she said, pulling the sports car over to the side of the little highway before motioning me toward a crude wooden fence, about chest high, made of split logs.

I leaped over a couple of puddles, climbed up the fence and perched on one splintery log.

She clicked a photo with the disposable camera and smiled.

"Now take one of me," she said. "Quick, before it goes away."

I glanced behind me and saw the rainbow hanging above us far away, brilliant as ever. I climbed down and took my place in front of the car as Lindsay clambered onto the fence and settled on a big thick log. She threw her arms up in a cheerleader-style "L," which she did a lot when posing for pictures. "L" was for "Lindsay," but in this case it also served to frame the rainbow. She flashed a big, bright smile.

I stood in front of the car and looked at her through the viewfinder. Her white T-shirt was still a little damp from when we'd gotten caught in the rain an hour before. I could see the contours of her firm tits and the peaks of her nipples, showing through the thin bra she wore. The spirals of lace accented the small mounds. Her khaki shorts, reaching to mid-thigh, were similarly damp, revealing the outline of her body as they hung low, beltless, on the swell of her hips.

"Any day now," she said.

"Just a sec," I said, savoring the view of her with her the shape of her nipples exposed, her strawberry-blonde hair damp with long-ago rain. I smiled.

"What's the holdup?" she asked.

"Take off your shirt."

Her skin, pink at all times, grew pinker still. "This is a public road."

"Exactly. Take off your shirt."

She thought about it for a moment, then whipped off her white T-shirt. Her perfect tits looked incredible, their curves revealed through the thin mesh with its spray of opaque lace at the bottoms.

I snapped a couple of pictures. I could see Lindsay blushing, but after the first few I could also tell she was enjoying herself. When she flashed her smiling "L" again to capture the rainbow, the white T-shirt slipped from her hand.

"Now the shorts," I told her.

"What? You *are* crazy."

"You have to change your shirt anyway. Might as well change everything."

"I don't have another clean pair," she said.

"I do," I told her. I moved the camera to the side and mouthed "Please?"

After a moment, she hooked her feet between the split logs of the crude fence and, without unzipping them, snugged her shorts down over her hips. Underneath she wore the skimpiest thong I'd ever seen. White mesh, totally see-through, showing her strawberry-blonde pubic hair.

"Very nice," I said as she spread her legs just enough to pause the shorts around her knees. "I especially like the fact that you're still wearing your hiking boots. That's sexy."

The shutter clicked.

She went to pull the shorts up and I said: "Uh-uh. Take them all the way off."

"This is getting ridiculous," she said.

"What have you got to lose?" I asked her.

"A couple hundred dollars for an indecent exposure citation?" she said.

"I'll pay it," I told her. "Please?"

Her hands were quivering as she lowered her khaki shorts

further, slipping them over her ankles. She looked awkwardly at the shorts.

"Toss them to me," I said.

Looking guilty, she tossed me the shorts and I caught them neatly, tossing them through the open driver's side window without looking back. I clicked the shutter and Lindsay made movements like she was starting to get down.

"I'm not finished with you," I said. "Take off the bra."

Maybe she had passed the point of no return; maybe her arousal was clouding her judgement. She didn't argue, just looked at me with a need for reassurance.

"You're sure?"

"It'll be all right," I said. "Show me your tits."

She glanced back at the rainbow. It was still there, gleaming brilliantly.

"Quick," I said. "Before the rainbow goes away."

She unhitched the front clasp of her bra and peeled the moist see-through mesh away from her gorgeous tits. Her nipples were very hard, now, and very pink. Like her face. She smiled and made her "L," and I could see her hands were shaking a little. It wasn't that cold.

"This is turning you on," I said, before I looked through the viewfinder and clicked.

"Yeah, I guess," she said, looking embarrassed. She thought about it for an instant, and I saw her eyes dart back toward the rainbow.

"Enough to get you wet?"

"I'm already wet," she said, running her hands through her dripping hair.

"You know what I'm talking about," I said, clicking the shutter.

"Yeah," she said. "I do."

"Are you?"

"I don't know."

"Touch your pussy and find out."

Again, the eyes flickering toward the rainbow. Her legs inching open, her fingers traveling tentatively up her thighs, then slipping down the small triangle of her thong. Her lips parted and she drew a sharp intake of breath as she touched her pussy.

"Are you?" I asked again.

She seemed beyond words. "Uh-huh," she said. She hadn't taken her hand out of her underwear. On the contrary, she was rubbing her pussy slowly, up and down, obviously not wanting to stop. "I'm...I'm going to get splinters in my butt."

I took four or five pictures in rapid succession of Lindsay rubbing herself with her hand tucked deep into that skimpy thong.

"We can't have that," I said. "Come down off the fence."

She still clutched her wet bra in her hand, and she didn't even notice when she dropped it as she climbed down. I tossed the camera into the car. Lindsay inched toward me, nervously, her eyes locked on mine. She didn't seem to mind that it had started to mist again. The rainbow began to wash away, but still hung there through the descending haze.

"Hi," she said shyly, as if she wasn't sure exactly what I intended to do.

When she was in grabbing distance I seized her, spun her around, and pushed her up against the hood of the car with her mouth molded to mine. She whimpered as my tongue slipped inside her mouth, and her arms went around me for just long enough to pull me close—then she was groping at my belt, pulling it open, unzipping my pants.

I placed her firmly on the tiny hood of the sports car and spread her out, legs wide as I plucked her thong out of the way. She got my cock, hard and ready, in her hand and guided it to her pussy. She moaned as I entered her.

The mist was really coming down, now, soaking us both, making Lindsay's naked flesh glisten with droplets. Her eyes flickered toward the remnants of the rainbow and then closed tight in hunger as she opened her mouth for mine, our tongues twisting together savagely. Her hands slid down into my pants and past the waistband of my shorts. She gripped my ass firmly, her nails digging in as she drew me deeper into her cunt.

The mist became a downpour. Lindsay spread her legs further and cinched her thighs around me, capturing me firmly. I leaned fully onto her, so much so that the car sank into the mud. I didn't care. I fucked her in long, quick strokes, making her pull me closer and sigh. Her hands gripped my hair as she sought purchase to lift her hips and meet my thrusts. Soon she was whimpering again, rhythmically this time, and I knew she was going to come.

It was a cloudburst, now, great warm droplets pumping onto us. There was so much water running down my face I could only see Lindsay through a great, blurry mass in flashes of brilliant lightning. She was moaning loud, really loud, her sounds shrouded in the roar of thunder and the rush of water.

My mouth seized her nipple and she arched her back as I began to suckle it. My fingers pressed 'round her face and she sucked desperately at my fingers as I plunged into her again and again. When she came, I felt her nails digging into my flesh—there would be marks. As her orgasm took her, her face exploded in a shimmer of lightning, illuminated by the flashing of the clouds. She screamed at the top of her lungs, a bestial release of energy that the storm and the thunder swallowed up like nothing. When I let myself go inside her, she whispered "Yes, yes, yes," close to my ear, and for some reason I could hear that over the rain.

We were both as wet, now, as if we'd been swimming. Me in my clothes, Lindsay in the smallest and most see-through thong bikini the law would allow and a big pair of tomboy hiking boots.

"Shit," I said, having difficulty talking because water was running into my mouth. "We'd better go before the mud swallows our car.

She ran to the passenger's side, forgetting her bra. She reached for the blanket we kept in the back seat, curling up under it, water and mud running everywhere. I jumped in and started the car, spinning the wheels before managing to pull out of the mud.

"The rainbow's gone," she said, looking sadly up into the sky where our patron saint had been suspended a half-hour ago, watching and tempting us.

"It'll be back," I said.

"Yeah," Lindsay answered thoughtfully. Then she smiled. "I think it will."

Too Shy...
by Ayre Riley

Josh works the register at the local grocery store, and I can't get my eyes off him. Dark hair, dark eyes, a goatee on his chiseled face. That face—like El Diablo—is hard as stone. I picture him staring at me as we fuck, those deep eyes watching me, those full lips parted and ravenous. I can see exactly the way it will be, but I don't know how to get us there.

He wears leather, black jeans, Docs. He has piercings and wrist bands and everything about him screams danger. In fact, he's just my type. Each time I see him, I feel that leg-weakening shudder start from deep inside me, and I have to hold onto the edge of my cart, or simply stand still and breathe deeply, which can look odd when you're in a rush-hour packed supermarket filled with people in a hurry. I don't care. I only have eyes for him.

But when, after weeks of staring, I finally get up the nerve to hand over my phone number along with the money for my groceries, he blushes. *What's up?* I wonder. He looks tougher than tough, yet I've managed to confuse him somehow with my scrap of paper and unlisted digits. He doesn't say a word as he tucks the paper into his front jeans pocket. Doesn't say anything as he hands over my change. Is he all looks and no play? I hope not. Back at home, I wish desperately that he'll come through for me. And my wishes are answered. He manages to call.

Yet even though he says he's been watching me as much as I've been watching him, waiting for me to choose his line with my cart of groceries, we find ourselves in an awkward situation, one that I've never experienced before. After work, he brings over a movie to watch with me, and I'm desperate to forget the onscreen action and create a little sofa action of our own. But the thing of it is this: We're too shy to act on our arousal. Can you believe that? I'm the girl who has actually picked up another date while on a date. I've done threesomes and foursomes, and yet with Josh I'm a virgin. I can't even remember how to kiss. What the rules are. Who goes where. How to get from up at bat to a home run. So fucking— well, that's so far out of the question that I can't even comprehend the concept.

This doesn't mean there isn't fire between us, because there is. Sparks. Heat. Volcanic lava. I come that night with my fingers against my clit, imagining what it will feel like when we ultimately do it. I know he has it in him. I can sense the passion waiting— repressed, but waiting. I make a promise to myself, that the next time, we'll just get down to business. Screw awkward pauses. Screw polite conversation. Screw each other.

Doesn't happen.

When we get together at his apartment, an innocence takes over that is so cute I can't stand it. He holds my hand and powerful trembles work through me. He runs his fingers over my jeans-clad thigh, and I think that I just might come from that touch alone. But that's all there is. Gentle, through-the-clothing stroking while our eyes remain focused on the TV screen.

The next weekend, another night goes by when all we do is sit side by side on his battered old sofa and watch films. Maybe, he's not really into me, I decide. Maybe, his looks are a facade. All toughness on the surface. Nothing beneath. But this time when I get home, there's a phone message.

"Hey lady," he says, "When you come over tomorrow tonight—and I *want* you to come over tomorrow night—don't be bringing no movies—"

So he feels what I feel. And even though we start off too shy, we get through that initial barrier. His hands on me, his arms around me, naked bodies pressed to bodies. He rips off his own clothes in record time, tosses me down on the bed, and I experience the fantasies I've had for weeks all together in one fresh rush of power and pleasure. His cock is so hard, and so ready, but he doesn't give in to his own needs right away. Instead, he slides his way down my body with the full, softness of his open mouth, and when he reaches the split between my legs, he goes to work.

I've never felt pleasure like that. Not ever. He moves his face gently back and forth between my thighs as his tongue traces designs up and over my clit. His soft goatee tickles my most tender skin. I grip into his thick dark hair and push him down on me, but he shrugs off my hands, not wanting to be rushed. "Hold onto the bed frame," he tells me, "or I'll have to tie you."

And now I'm getting everything I want, everything I knew that he had to give. With his leather, and his laces, and his wristcuffs and silver rings. With his tattoos and his dead-eyed stare for customers who are annoying him. He is all that power, confined in one beautiful body, and he bestows every cell of himself to giving me pleasure. He holds onto my waist as he brings his tongue up and down between the split of my lips. Then he goes back and forth again, and I'm lost.

I come twice on his tongue, and then, just to see if he means what he says, I let go of the railing. In an instant, he has me bound to the bedframe with leather thongs, and my hips start to thrash on the bed. I want him inside me, and he's finally ready to give in to me. Climbing on top of me, he fucks me hard and steady, his thumbs parting my nether lips as he slides in deep. He tricks his fingers over the split of my body, and he makes me come again. Come until I am whimpering, until I can do nothing but sigh.

"Don't know what happened to me," he whispers afterward, face pressed into my long black hair. "I'm usually so take-charge. But you had me off-balance. Didn't want to rush. Didn't want to ruin it. Couldn't even get up the nerve to ask you out, so I'm lucky that you forced the issue."

Crazy, right?

Too shy to talk to me, but not—thank God—to fuck.

Made to Order
by Rachel Kramer Bussel

"Touch yourself for me, make yourself come." She barked it out, in her haughty British accent, with nary a thought as to what my reaction would be. She said it with total assurance and coolness, no "I want you to" or "Please" to preface the statement, the way I would have. This tone suited her though, and I should've expected it after picking her up at a sex party, all decked out in slick, shiny, black rubber and spike-heel boots. She looked like a dominatrix, partly because of the clothes, but even more so because of her posture and the sneering look on her face. The way she sat and surveyed the room, and then me, told me that she was the kind of girl who could get anything she wanted, and usually did.

She was my type though; I liked feisty women who could throw me off guard, titillate me into confusion. I didn't want someone meek like me; the pair of us would probably never get past holding hands. Though I was drawn to her, I was a little afraid of her, or maybe I just wanted to be afraid of her. Either way, I wanted to please her.

There was something in her tone, the way she commanded me like she knew without a doubt that I'd obey, that made me *want* to obey. Her request made me reconsider masturbation as a one-woman show. Sure, other lovers had asked that I do the same, but they'd always followed up their request with a girlish set of giggles, letting me know that it was as amusing to them as it sounded to me. They seemed to make the request just to hear the words echo in the air, presuming they'd set off a sudden erotic chain reaction. But she succeeded, turning me on with the idea that my pussy was enough to get both of us off.

I did as she requested, lying back, closing my eyes in an attempt to be slightly less aware of her direct gaze, which spared me nothing in its appraisal. I wouldn't have chosen this form of sex, would've preferred something a bit more mutual, more sensual. I was worried

I wouldn't be able to come, that touching myself wouldn't be the same with her watching. Maybe I could fake it? No, that wouldn't do either; I was too on edge.

My index and middle fingers worked my clit, parting the hood and rubbing, rubbing, gently, then faster and faster. I tried up and down, then a circle, rocking against my fingers to increase the pressure. I tried to relax, to let my whole body sink into the bed, to focus all my energy on my clit. My breath started coming out in quick pants, almost getting stuck in my throat. I didn't have energy to waste on breathing, only on my restless, relentless fingers.

I resisted the urge to move closer to her, to rub myself against her, to cuddle in the warmth of her skin. There'd be plenty of time for that later. I shut my eyes harder and shoved my fingers inside my pussy, then pulled them out and returned to my clit.

"Do it the way you do when you're alone, at home."

I almost laughed at that, because at home I rely on my trusted vibrator to do this work for me, and all my hand has to do is make sure the toy doesn't fall. I'd stopped using my hand the moment I found my first vibrator and hadn't returned. So this was a bit of a reacquaintance for my hand and my cunt. I tried to go back to the pre-vibrator times, when my fingers and imagination had been my sole guides.

She kept me pinned with her eyes, with her spoken request that I not get up before I came. She didn't try to come herself or even appear visibly moved by my actions, but I could sense that her pleasure lay in her power to command me to come, to make me make myself get off, to fall apart and resurrect myself while she calmly looked on.

"That's it, now come for me. I need to watch you, to see your face when you reach that magic moment. Come!" She was close to screaming the last word, and sounded like she needed the release more than I did. Her voice carried such force, like she was the Queen of the Universe, or at least, my bedroom. She spoke like she was *made* to order me around, to command me to come. In turn, I was there to obey, to fulfill her every wish.

I rubbed my clit even more frantically, calling out as I reached the point where I couldn't stop even if I'd wanted to. My fingers moved almost of their own accord, in a race with my clit to push me over the edge, into the fiery chill of orgasm, when my body barely knows what direction it's going in and I could be anywhere on earth. My eyes closed and small teardrops formed at the edges, mimicking the liquid that began to build inside me. As I teetered, she must have been staring, close enough to judge my arousal. All of a sudden, she yanked sharply on my hair, sending a wave of heat and pain and pleasure from my scalp shooting down to my cunt. As she pulled, I came, the liquid evidence pouring out of me.

I quivered and shook, loving the way my orgasm led itself throughout my body, leaving me tender and aroused. She kissed my pussy, gently, like a pat on the head for a job well done. I wrapped my legs around her meaty thigh, burrowed into her neck, and went to sleep.

Two Thumbs Up
(The Perfect Date)

by Iris N. Schwartz

It was to be their third date, and Therese had said: "I want you to remember it always." Gerard had asked her where she wanted to go that night, and had readily agreed to her less-than-scintillating suggestion: dinner and a movie. He'd agreed because of who Therese was: it didn't matter if they sucked down soup at a local grease-o-rama—he was always at ease with and excited by this woman.

Gerard didn't want to assume tonight would be the night he'd score: he'd enjoyed too many years and too many women to assume anything. Oh, she was sexy, this Therese, this sister-in-academe, with black hair that brushed strong shoulders, full, always-lipsticked lips, and eyes as dark as the chocolate she'd licked off her fingers near the end of last Saturday's date. Plus, she talked as well as Gerard, sometimes employing words he'd never heard, and had divulged feelings that rivaled the deepest he'd ever felt. Gerard understood Therese was no one to toy with. This left his desire only slightly tainted with respect.

When they'd first started flirting, at a restaurant five blocks from the campus where both taught, Gerard had imparted to Therese several fantasies—role-playing in a doctor's office, escapades involving paddles or whips—and she'd lowered her eyes twice but then asked him for more. Gerard had been drunk when he'd waxed lascivious, but Therese hadn't been, and as the night lengthened she'd responded with fantasies of tickling with emu feathers, restraining limbs with silk scarves, and other scenarios he deemed mild but inviting.

He longed for her to open up even more. They'd been on two dates since that evening at the restaurant, and had kissed four times altogether, but what kisses: penetrating and moist, exquisite affairs of melding lips and conjoined tongues.

Gerard got hard each time he closed his eyes and remembered.

He wondered if she would pull back now, scared by this earlier sex talk, thus returning them to the start of the game. The thing was, Therese would be good company even if she *didn't* put out, and he knew damn well she knew it.

So he picked her up at seven and they scurried off to a romantic Italian inn, the kind women love and, frankly, the kind Gerard himself favored, with linen tablecloths and artful floral arrangements, suffused lighting and fireplace in the rear. Hell, if Therese weren't here, he'd romance *himself*. This place was *good*. Gerard felt he had much to offer: as a sociology professor, little money; nonetheless, he spilled forth wit, intelligent conversation, stamina and generosity in bed. He was in his early forties, and still handsome enough to turn heads. Certainly his own, in his mirror, at home. Certainly Therese's. And when he enjoyed a woman, as he did Therese, he might get down on his knees and thank God for a chance to please her.

Gerard was getting serious. He didn't want to get serious. He felt buoyant and hopeful right now. He didn't know how he'd do tonight, but just in case he had worn his new briefs, his royal blues, the ones that made him feel studly. The ones that accentuated his compact, taut-muscled buttocks, that highlighted a winning penile profile, that afforded a woman full frontal royal blue bliss. Ah, King Stud. *Professor* Stud. And women liked him in this color, said it complemented the grey streaks in his head of still-thick brown hair, Gerard's *next*-to-finest feature.

Tonight Therese was sipping wine with dinner. She hadn't drunk wine with him before. Maybe Therese would loosen up more, maybe she'd giggle again. Gerard enjoyed the way her eyes narrowed when she laughed, the way she lowered those eyes and nibbled her lips when she talked with him about sex.

They were discussing a study he was reading, about the effects of broken parental bonds on later forms of intimacy, as well as the ramifications for society as a whole. He didn't mind the topic— truly, it was one of his favorites—but it made for an ever-so-slightly scholarly time here at this candle-lit joint. Still, Therese seemed at ease, even playful, at one point buttering and feeding him his bread, and he didn't want to push her.

When they arrived at the theater, Therese insisted on seats in the back, on the left next to the wall, though there were many empty rows ahead. Well, Gerard had no reason to object. Maybe she wanted to make out and didn't desire a crowd. He was sensitive enough to appreciate that.

Previews appeared and Gerard offered popcorn from the bag in his lap. Would Therese dive in or ask him to pass the popcorn? This dating litmus test proved almost 100% accurate in predicting success or the lack for the night. Therese, however, declined the snack altogether. Was she watching her weight, turning cold, or—smart woman—on to his lecherous ways? Could be it was time to stop interpreting. Could be it was time to sit back and relax.

A minute or so into the movie, with the titles still rolling, Therese whispered that she had a surprise. Why now? The theater was quiet. He didn't want to speak. Gerard squinted at her and cocked his head, but she simply smiled and took his left hand with her right. The sociology professor stared at the figures onscreen but his thoughts were with Therese.

Just as the last filmgoer settled in, Gerard felt her glide his hand up her leg. Oh, this was nice. He met sheer nylon, the bone of her knee, then more ample, still-stockinged flesh. With Therese's hand guiding his, he stroked her full lower thighs.

Damn, give him a *lifetime* of surprises. He heard the beating of his heart, like his own movie score, and heralded the heat in his loins, a private sense-a-rama in blue briefs. Suddenly there was skin—bare, cool, soft skin—and without looking Gerard knew she wasn't wearing panties. Before he could say *heaven*, his hand was cupping dewy folds of flesh, lips as luscious as the full ones on her face. Slowly, slowly, his middle finger circled, caressed, enveloped her clitoris.

For all the talk, all the music, all the light emanating from the screen, all Gerard knew was his hand centered in this one perfect place. All he heard was her husky breathing beside him. And, of course, the never-quiet voice of his own royal-blue enclosed cock, straining to be set free.

The professors turned to one another simultaneously, the words of the first almost eclipsing those of the second.

"I'm usually not one for surprises," he breathed into her ear. And from her, "I thought you might like *this* surprise."

They laughed quietly. Therese's eyes were shut. For the first time Gerard turned to see if anyone was looking their way. The theatre doors were closed, most rows ahead still empty. Everyone else seemed content with the film. Fools: just last week he would have felt the same, but nothing, not even *9-1/2 Weeks,* rivaled the action in their seats.

With that, Gerard removed his hand and stood up slowly. "Don't worry," he said *sotto voce,* "I'm not going anywhere," and with that he knelt in front of her seat. She opened her lovely eyes wide and stared.

"Hey, baby," he spoke into her pink, "you started." Too bad he couldn't get an usher's flashlight. *Excuse me,* he'd say, *I believe I dropped my keys.*

Gerard slid a finger inside, moved it amidst her softness, slowly. She was slick, as slick as he himself was hard. When he removed his finger and inserted it in her mouth, she licked it, thirsty puppy, and asked him to do it again. He put in two fingers then, and the next time, three. Each time she sighed and opened wider, each time sucking her juices off his slippery digits.

Inside Gerard's pants lived an elephantine bulge, and he hoped she'd relieve him soon. Who knew *where* the relief would come— in a parking lot, perhaps, or if that was too *empty,* by the salad bar in a delicatessen?

Therese held Gerard's head in place. He hoped there'd be no one cruising these aisles anytime soon. Now he had his thumbs inside Therese and both pointers lightly flicking her clitoris. She was writhing in her chair—he'd bet she'd *soaked* that goddamned chair—but was so quiet he didn't need to cover her mouth. Still, he kissed her a few times, both to maintain that silence and to feel his tongue inside another receptive orifice. He wished he'd had a larger part of him inside her, but this would do for now.

He was still kneeling before her and with his tongue began to flit around and then atop her clit. That's when he felt her buck in the chair. That's when he saw her squeeze her breasts. And that's when he thought he heard feet in the aisle, but it was her, kicking the chair in front. Someone yelled "Shush!" and someone else said "Hey!" Gerard asked Therese to stop, but she couldn't. He grabbed her legs before they made contact again.

"I'm sorry, God, I'm sorry," she panted into his ear. Gerard didn't know which he liked more, making her come or hearing her address him as a higher power.

I'm not sorry. From now on, I'll beg for surprises. He saw Therese bite her lower lip, then grin. He hadn't realized he'd spoken aloud.

Gerard kissed her on the earlobe. "So, where do we go for dessert?" Therese grabbed Gerard's still damp hand and slowly rose from her chair. "I don't care," she shook her head and smiled, "as long as it's you."

Shaved

by Christopher Wilson

She knows it's going to happen tonight. It scares her, the idea of having a sharp instrument so close to her pussy. But what scares her excites her.

Years ago, I invested in an old gynecological table I found at a junk sale. I replaced the badly-designed stirrups with better ones that would accept restraints. I bought a metal drill and put eyebolts in the sides for wrist restraints. I covered it in black leather. I added an eyebolt, too, for a collar, for when I want to keep Kathleen really immobile.

Now, the table is in our playroom, in the basement. I turned the heat on in the afternoon so it'll be nice and warm. After dinner, I tell her to go down and get dressed.

Whenever Kathleen enters the dungeon, she can expect that I will have laid out her clothes for her. Tonight it's something very special. She's still wearing her work clothes, so I know her businesslike white lace panties will be moist from anticipation. And they'll only get wetter when she sees what I've chosen.

It's slutty: the kind of slutty outfit that will fit perfectly on a shaved whore. Except she's not shaved yet.

She strips off her business clothes, piling them neatly in the corner. She climbs into the see-through leopard-print camisole, no doubt noting how stretchy it is, how it cradles her firm D-cup breasts. Her nipples poke straight through. She puts on the matching leopard-print G-string and obediently sits on the table and waits.

When I come down, I'm holding a basin of hot water and a straight razor. Her eyes are wide as she looks at the razor. I set the tools down on the table next to her; then I padlock her wrists and ankles to the eyebolts of the table. Her legs are spread very wide.

Kathleen looks at me, frightened and aroused. I lean forward and kiss her neck beneath her blonde hair, then kiss up to her mouth and plunge my tongue into her. I reach down and feel her cunt through the thin, stretchy material of the G-string. It's very wet, the G-string soaked already.

I take the digital camera from the table. I snap a few pictures of her cunt, untouched and covered in fine, dark hair underneath the see-through panties. The fine hair tufts out around the edges of the panties' crotch. I don't get her face; that's our agreement. I can photograph my slave's pussy, ass and tits all I want, but her face remains hidden.

Kathleen's pussy hair is thick black, a silent testament to her Italian heritage and the fact that she bleaches her hair. I was partial to brunettes when I met her, and she was a pale-skinned brunette, her hair coal-black and lustrous; the moment she bleached her hair blonde I developed a preference for goldilocks. Still, I have to admit that seeing her naked makes it painfully obvious that she's a bottle blonde.

But that's not why I'm shaving her. I actually like the black hair, reminding me every time I see her pussy that I know a secret about my willing submissive, my obedient slave, my wife.

No, I'm shaving her for a simple reason. I've never fucked a bare pussy, and I want to try one out. A sharp blade so close to Kathleen's pussy makes her incredibly wet; that's just the icing on the cake.

Kathleen moans as she feels the cold metal of the razor against her thigh. As I kiss her on the lips, my tongue savaging her, I neatly slit the sides of the G-string and pull it off of her cunt, its meshy material rubbing her clit as I lift it and run her panties over her face. She smells herself, smells how wet she is.

I take two more pictures, these of her naked cunt, its hair unkempt and full.

It's time. I pump the hot lather dispenser and feel the warm, soft gush flowing into my palm.

I lather her up and look into her eyes as the hot soap covers her pussy.

She holds very still, her lips trembling as she watches me softening her pussy hair with the soap. The first scrape of the razor against her upper thighs makes her hold her breath. The second makes her bite her tongue. When I tug her labia out and gently start to shave them smooth, I see her eyes go wide.

When I'm finished with her labia, I move to the untrimmed thatch above her pussy. I tease her opening and feel how wet it is. I bend forward and kiss her.

I slowly draw the razor over Kathleen's pubic thatch, scraping her clean. I dip the razor in hot water and add more hot lather between each stroke. I'm very careful not to slip at all.

When I reach out for the hot towel and rub it over her pussy, she moans.

When I draw the towel away, she looks down and sees her pussy bare and smooth. Hairless.

She's breathing very hard. I hold up a mirror and she stares, as if she can't believe it's her pussy.

I dry my hands, take up the camera again, and take new pictures of my wife's pussy, revealed utterly. I show Kathleen the pictures of her shaved pussy on the digital screen. She stares, amazed. I feel her pussy and find it still quite wet.

I unzip my pants and take out my rock-hard cock. I know she'll be extra sensitive, and that the sensitivity will excite her.

Kathleen struggles against her restraints as I insert my cock into her shaved pussy. The bareness makes it smooth, slick, and I feel her wriggle as the ultrasensitized flesh of her cunt reacts to each stroke. Soon she's whimpering and gasping, each thrust bringing a noise of surprise from her lips. That makes me fuck her harder, which makes her moan.

The whole length of my cock feels alive, teased into vibrant sensation by the new smoothness of Kathleen's shaved pussy. I bend forward and kiss her as I sense her getting close to her orgasm, and then she twists and pulls against the bonds; I hear her come as I pump her faster, bringing myself closer to my own climax. When I come, she pulls violently against the bonds, thrashing as she tries to pump her hips up harder to take my cock deeper. I flood her freshly shorn cunt with my come, and she nuzzles her face against mine as she surrenders her newly smooth pussy to me.

I take several more pictures as my come starts to leak out of her shaved pussy. She looks at the camera and I sense something special about the way she's looking. Slowly, I turn the camera up to her face. She looks right into it, smiles, and nods.

I pull the viewfinder back so I can get her come-dripping, shaved pussy, her gorgeous leopard-print-clad breasts, and her breathtaking face so fetchingly framed by her blonde hair. All in one shot. I can see her smiling wickedly, her wrists and arms bound and her pussy shaved, as she gives up this one last boundary, letting me photograph her face and pussy in one shot.

I know she could ask me to erase the picture later—and I know I will comply. But something tells me she won't, that I'll have this photograph of my wife to savor forever. Her face, her tits, and her cunt—shaved and filled with my come. A picture of love, cherished forever. My wife, shaved not just of her hair, but of her last inhibitions. Surrendering to me, totally.

And it's the most beautiful picture I've ever taken.

"I Do"
by Eric Caldwell

I was best man at my friend's wedding. Standing there, dressed in a tux and tails, sweltering in the heat of the non-air-conditioned hall, I couldn't think of a place I'd less like to be... until I realized that one of the bridesmaids was making eyes at me. These incredible, baby blue goo-goo eyes. I stopped praying for the thing to be finished and started paying attention to the beautiful doll all dressed up in creamy taffeta.

She had that pale yellow hair that looks like duck down, soft and fine as baby's hair. For the event, it was braided against her skull, but a few of those wisps had already gotten free. I longed to undo the braids and let loose her tresses, pictured myself sitting behind her on a bed—any bed, *my* bed—and drawing a boar-bristle brush through her long mane.

I almost missed my cue when I was supposed to pass over the rings, lost as I was in the vision nearby. Then, in answer to my unspoken wishes, the service was suddenly over and people were rushing forward to offer their congratulations.

My lush miss was lost in the crowd for a moment, but I found her, being hugged and kissed and having her hand shaken in the reception line.

"Can I borrow you for a second?" I asked, disregarding the looks from those around me. "Important wedding business," I added, trying to sound dignified.

She gave me one more of those "melt-me-please" looks and then followed me to the back of the church.

"Who are you?" I demanded. She hadn't been at the rehearsals.

"Cousin of the bride," she said, softly, sweetly, tilting her head down in that adorable way many subs do, and pulling gently on the lace of her dress.

"Aren't you hot in that?" I asked next, steering her, as I spoke, to the room where the bride had gotten ready.

She nodded, still in that bashful way, allowing herself to be led to the room, and then further back, to the bathroom. It was in speeded-up motion that I freed her from the off-white fluff gown and got her down to her lace bra and panty set. She had an incredible figure, once revealed, curved where it was supposed to be curved, slender in the slenderest places. Her breasts were full and lovely in my mouth. Her scent wafted up around us until I couldn't wait anymore and peeled her panties down her thighs, plunging my hungry tongue deep into her wet pussy.

There was a mirror on the back of the bathroom door, and I angled us so that she could watch me eat her. I checked to make sure her eyes were on the mirror, that they never strayed, and she, understanding my desire, obeyed.

She had drenched her thighs during the service, and I spent a good long time licking her clean, then parting her thighs even wider and dipping my head to get a taste of the split between her legs, to reach my tongue back to tickle her asshole.

That made her moan and grab onto my hair, and I quickly turned her so that she was bent over the sink and began reaming her with my thumb and forefinger. The noises she made were divine, and *loud*, and before I could stop her, before I could remind her where we were, she was moaning, "Yes, oh, yes, oh yes."

That little voice in the back of my head, that little sane voice that I often try to stamp out, was saying, "Hush. Get back in the receiving line. Fix her up and get her out before you're caught."

But I couldn't. Instead, squashing that sane little voice, I undid my slacks and freed my cock and said, "Do you want this, honey?" Rubbing it up against her moist slit, probing her with it. "Do you want this, darling? Do you want this?"

And she bent over forward, offering herself to me completely, as she moaned, over and over, in a voice that grew loud enough for the entire congregation to hear... "I do!"

Tess Needs a Spanking
N.T. Morley

Tess needs a spanking. She really, really needs a spanking. She needs it so bad she keeps wriggling her ass back and forth, asking for it, begging for it. She doesn't even know she's doing it; it's like her ass has a mind of its own, squirming and fidgeting under that tight skirt as she walks past me or bends over within sight of me. She needs it so bad she's wet under her skirt; her pussy is swollen and tight, aching and hungry to feel the sting on her ass as she shakes back and forth, sobbing and crying. She needs it so bad she keeps messing up, bringing me the wrong file, the wrong document, spilling my coffee, forgetting the cream.

But I don't need an excuse to spank Tess.

Tess doesn't even know how bad she needs a spanking. She never does, not until I grab her by the waist and tumble her over my lap; not until I grasp her by the hair and push her face into the crook of my arm and tell her to pull her skirt up over her round cheeks and take down her panties. She never knows how bad she needs a spanking until after I've pulled her skirt up myself, found out how wet she is under her tight lace thong, discovered the squeals that come out of her mouth when I rub her wet pussy and slide two fingers inside. She never knows how bad she needs a spanking until after I've given her one, open-handed, spanking her ass rhythmically, first one cheek and then the other, right on the sweet spot and occasionally in the middle, right over her pussy. She never knows how bad she needs a spanking until after she's started to lift her ass in the air, pump it hungrily in long, slow circles, shake back and forth and wet my suit with tears. She never knows how bad she needs a spanking until after she buries her face in my arm, spreads her legs, and grips the legs of the chair tightly to steady herself as I beat her. She never knows until after she's cried, whimpered, cajoled, tried to bargain, tried to threaten, tried to wriggle her way out of one. She never knows until after she's started to moan. She never knows until she's felt it building deep in her cunt, felt the blows driving all the way into her luscious little snatch and punishing her throbbing clitoris. Still, until that very last moment, no matter how many times it happens, she clings to her resistance, adheres to her passionate belief that she's done nothing wrong, that she *doesn't* need a spanking and if she whines and cries and complains, I'll see the light and just *stop*. But I don't, and it's a good thing for her, because the only time I give her one is when she really, truly, desperately, urgently needs a spanking.

But Tess never knows how bad she needs a spanking until after she's thrown back her head and pushed her ass high into the air and *come*, overwhelmed by the profound satisfaction of having her need satisfied, the deep need for what, if she had been allowed to have her way, she never would have gotten.

But luckily, Tess has me to tell her when she *does* need a spanking. And once she's had one, she always does exactly what she knows she needs to do.

Which is pull down her panties and put her ass in the air, and await another spanking—this one for saying *no*.

And afterwards, she takes a moment to fix her hair, put her soaked panties back on, straighten her skirt. Then she returns to her work, and for the rest of the day, she never, ever brings me the wrong file or forgets the cream in my coffee.

Because she's forgotten, the moment she finished, how badly she needs a spanking.

But she'll remember. Oh, she'll remember. And each time she'll forget most deliciously.

The Runner
by Barbara Fields

You've seen us before. I know you have. We're difficult to miss, clad in our shining, skin-tight outfits, pumping our taut muscles as we cut through the cool air of the morning. You've watched us from the safety of your car during your early morning commute, watched rather lecherously as our thighs power up the hilly trail that winds along next to the highway. And I'll bet you've even touched the black leggings in the sports store, running your fingers over that lightweight fabric, imagining the blue swash of color poured down the center of a pair of particularly fine female legs. Never thought sports gear would turn you on, did you?

It's okay to admit it. It's okay to state the obvious. You can't hide from me. I've seen you watching me, seen you, with your traveler's mug filled with some high-end designer coffee, your eyes still partially glazed with sleep, watching me and my friends climb the trail. Route 280 is a gorgeous drive through California countryside, but you have eyes only for my calves, my ass, my thighs.

I have a job, same as you do. I could be in the car next to yours, my own java mug in hand, my own eyes heavy with lack of sleep and lack of exercise. Instead, I get up early and power the hills. Then head to work and stay there late, the energy still riding in my bloodstream from my early morning run. I do it because it's healthy and it gives me energy. And, since you admitted your addiction to my thighs, I will admit my addiction to your eyes. I like to be watched when I wear my work clothes, my finely-cut suit adhering perfectly to my toned form. I don't dress in a risque manner, it wouldn't be appropriate to my occupation, but I do choose my attire carefully, knowing my legs are my strong point.

And you like them, don't you? As you sip your mug and wait in the stifling boredom of the morning traffic. You like the way my honed form keeps you entertained. You've picked me to watch, out of my female companions. You've picked me for my wave of cinnamon hair that floats behind me like a banner. You've picked me because I sometimes turn and meet your eyes. There's not so much distance separating us. Asphalt, chrome, dirt. Not much separating us but my sleek seal-like lycra and your expensive black power suit. Not much separating us but my naked skin and my long hair, which picks up the scent of the morning air, and your body, slim and hard and ready.

I would like to touch you. I would like to run my hands along the tight flatness of your body, would like to learn your form the way I know my mountain, almost mindlessly moving my feet along the track I've run so many times before. I could memorize the map of your body to that extreme. I could learn where to touch you to bring you the most pleasure, where to put my hand, cupping it around your cock, my fingertips floating butterfly-light against your balls. I would like to curl up against a body that is so much different from mine.

I have muscle beneath the lycra leggings you see me wear. But I'm still curved. I would like you to cup my sweet breasts in your hands and touch your lips to my rosy nipples. Would like you to spread me out on the mattress and learn the dips and curves of my body. The indents. The places where I am soft, where I am wet. With your hard, action-ready body and my athletic shape, we could fit together easily. I know this. Easily as two pieces of a well-used puzzle. I have seen it in your eyes, as you peer out your windshield, wanting me.

I have wants, too.

Something Sweet
by Alison Tyler

Food is Jesse's life. When he cooks, he creates works of art. The reviews of his restaurant say that. It's not just me. I watch him shop. He buys for the color and the texture, as well as the taste. At home, he arranges fruit in white porcelain bowls. The cherries are ripe, so dark they look black. He puts one in my mouth, pulls the stem, smiles as I suck the sweet fruit away from the pit.

Often, he cooks for me. I sit at the counter while he cuts purple bell peppers over vibrant green salads, sprinkles crushed red cayenne over adobe-colored tortillas. He sets out our meals the way an artist would arrange a collage, moving and adjusting, creating the perfect array, an intense blend of food and art.

Jesse plays with me in the kitchen. He sets a bowl of cream on the black-and-white tiled floor, watches me crawl to it, lap from it. Lifting my thin, pink nightgown, he enters me from behind, pushing my face forward, getting my lips, tongue, and chin wet with the cream. A fist wrapped in my dark hair pulls back so my head comes up, and he bends forward to lick away the wetness. Then he lets me go, lets me bend on hands and knees and drink with tiny flicks of my tongue, taking in droplets of the sweet cream.

Cream. It's all about cream. He doesn't buy half and half. He doesn't buy powdered. He buys cartons of cream. The way most people buy milk. It's thick and rich and he pours it into a bowl for me, a blue glass bowl that he places carefully on the cold tiled floor.

"Make like a kitty," he says, coming around to kneel by my side, moving the bowl so that he can dip his cock into it, coat the tip of his cock and then sit back on his heels and let me lick it clean. "Be a good little kitty and drink it all up," he says, dipping his cock again and then waiting for my pink tongue to bathe him, to catch every drop. I don't suck him, I lick the cream away, lick each bit and watch him strain for it, yearning for my warm mouth.

Dip and lick. This game could go on forever. The cool cream

on his cock followed by the warm wet lick of my tongue. He dips his cock deeper into the bowl, pushing down on it with his fingertips so that the head and shaft are coated with the rich liquid. I wait for him to grab my hair again, to pull me down on him. This time I suck him. I take his cock down my throat, swallowing and tasting the cream and then the liquid that comes from him.

He grabs the bowl, moves it between his legs, dips down so that his balls skim the cream, stands up so that I can raise myself on just my knees to lick. I open my mouth and let him dip his balls again, this time coming to rest against my outstretched tongue.

When he's back on his knees, he takes my hair, pushes my face into the bowl, brings me up so he can kiss the cream from my lips, lick each drop as I have done. He pushes me down on my back on the tile floor. He lifts my nightgown to reveal my shaved pussy, pours the bowl of cream between my legs, holding my pussylips open with his fingers so that the stream of liquid falls in a rush over my clit.

He's the cat, now. Not a kitty, but a Tom cat, on hands and knees licking the wet milky white cream away, then making a different kind of cream rise to the surface. The bowl is forgotten. The pool of cream on the floor is slick and cool. My ass is wet, but it doesn't matter. All that matters is his tongue, the flat of his tongue against my cunt, running the length of it, from the opening between my legs to the pubic bone. Wetness forms on my inner lips. He holds them wide, licks away the moisture, the wet of his tongue making me wetter.

His mouth against my cunt, his lips around my clit, he sighs, pulls back, says, "You taste like cream." Licks again, mouth open, hungry, eating from me. I feed him. This pleases me. From my body, the juices of my body, I feed him.

Bella's Secret Garden
by Antonia Paris

One of my favorite things about staying in a hotel is the maid service. I can't tell you how luxurious it is to know that I won't have to pick up after myself, won't be required to fold the towels and place them on the rack when I'm through. My girlfriend, however, cannot get the hang of hotel life. She actually cleans our room before the maid arrives.

"I don't want her to think we're slobs," she says.

"That's her job," I tell her.

"To think we're slobs?" (An intentional misread. I want to smack her for it.)

"To clean up," I say through clenched teeth.

Amber shrugs, then makes the bed. When she's finished, she writes a note to the maid, places it with a five dollar bill on the dresser, and gets ready to go. I watch her but don't say anything. There's no point.

When we return from sightseeing, our maid has left us a note of her own. It says, "Thank you very much for the tip. You don't need to make the bed since I change the sheets every day." She's signed it Bella. I show the note to Amber who announces in her haughtiest tone that she doesn't care. She'll make the bed anyway.

The next day, it's raining and we stay in. Part of our vacation is just relaxing, which means we don't have to sightsee each and every day. Part of MY vacation, that is. Amber takes her camera, despite the rain, and leaves. I snooze until the maid knocks on the door. Then I stumble to the latch and open it. In the hallway, stands Bella. She's a pert and perfectly adorable blonde with short curly hair and clear, blue eyes. She takes one look at me and says, "You're not the one making the bed each day, are you?"

I shake my head and invite her in. Something in my look must let her know what I want, and she obliges. She's easy in my arms, a sweet 105-pounder with a lithe, athletic body. I kiss her mouth, then her freckled cheeks, then nibble on her earlobes. I move her with me into the bathroom and we take a shower together, getting warm and wet and soapy. Laughing as we dry each other off.

We leave the towels in a soggy heap on the floor and make it halfway to the bed before I grab her and throw her down on the plush, crimson carpeting that Amber has picked lint off on her hands and knees. I climb on top of Bella in a stilldamp sixty-nine. She knows how to use her tongue, probes me expertly with it while stroking my ass and lower back, rubbing in small circles, dragging her nails against my skin.

I follow her lead, running my short nails the length of her inner thighs while keeping my mouth busy on her cunt. I like the way she tastes, clean from the shower, of course, but musky beneath it. Earthy and real and delicious to my taste buds. Her fragrance is rich and heady and entirely unlike the antiseptic flavor of Amber's well-douched vagina. Amber doesn't really like it when we sixty-nine. She can eat me for hours, but she doesn't like me to go down on her.

I lap now at Bella with no thought of what she's doing to my own cunt. I am lost within the walls of her pussy, drinking each drop of her nectar. Finally, I pull away from her, lying flat on the floor between her legs, and concentrate totally on giving her pleasure. She wraps her thighs around me and lets me work, whispering what she wants, how she likes it. "Harder," when she needs that, "faster, ohhh, please, faster," and I make those spiraling little circles as quickly as I can until she presses her hips forward and drenches my lips with the juices of her climax. The taste is pure sweetness.

By the time Amber arrives, Bella and I are on our third beer. Amber doesn't know what to make of the scene, so I tell her. "You're doing Bella's job. Cleaning. Folding. Running around. So I invited her to do yours... kick back, hang out, make love."

Amber leaves with her very neatly folded clothes packed in her immaculate suitcase. Bella and I have another beer, then climb beneath the tightly, tucked sheets and relax.

Working Overtime
by Sage Vivant

David turned into the DermaCare Inc. driveway that Sunday with more than a little irritation. He could think of seven thousand things he'd rather be doing than picking up some equipment for a patient.

When he flicked on the office lights, he jumped at the sight that greeted him.

"I thought you'd never get here," Pauline purred. She wore a button-up dress that was unbuttoned to her navel, exposing a tempting slash of cleavage. She lay across the desk on her side, one hand propping up her head. Her grin was enormous.

"What the—"

She laughed loudly, pleased at her plan's success.

"How did you get in here?" he demanded, closing the door behind him.

"A determined woman has her methods. But this is no time for details." She lured him closer with a crook of her finger.

He approached, stopping at the edge of the desk. She moved her face closer to his crotch, which had already begun to balloon. She unzipped him with exceptional skill and had his excited member looking up at the fluorescent lights in seconds. Before he could speak, her mouth engulfed his grateful, purple head.

She crept closer to him very slowly, so that he disappeared in her hot mouth centimeters at a time. She sucked him as he entered, drawing him deeper into her throat. When she reached the base, she circled her tongue around his shaft and gradually slid him out of her mouth.

He gasped as she repeated the process, over and over again. He held her head with one hand and the edge of the desk with the other. Just as he thought he might explode between her talented lips, she squeezed his balls playfully and popped him out of her mouth.

"My pussy needs feeding more than my mouth does," she whispered. Sitting upright, she straddled him with her legs. She hiked up her skirt in the process, revealing a panty-less cunt, already shiny with her juices. Speech eluded him. He couldn't stop staring but had to when her furry heat touched the tip of his knob.

She guided his thick meat inside her. As her wet folds surrounded him, he moaned and closed his eyes. She supported herself with her hands behind her. He grabbed the breast that escaped her dress.

She controlled the pumping, slamming herself onto his swollen cock until he could restrain himself no longer. He gushed into her and heard her squealing her own pleasure as a key jiggled in the lock of the back door.

The couple froze but then launched into action. Pauline scrambled for her shoes and tried to smooth her hair. The door opened and in bounded Chuck, one of the company's drivers, who was working overtime, himself.

Chuck paused, registering either the scent or the aura in the room. "Hope I'm not interrupting anything." He seemed more embarrassed than they were.

"No, no. Pauline was just helping me with some equipment," David explained as the couple quickly exited.

Penance
by Rachel Kramer Bussel

"You're late."

He looks up at me with a contrite expression, but that's not enough for me now.

"And not only that, but you totally canceled on our last date." I'm tapping foot, encased in my five inch heel, and holding the riding crop by my side, my anger spilling out into my voice. "Strip. Yes, right now, get going, then get down on your hands and knees. You don't deserve to stand today. Don't even look at me like you don't know what's wrong or like you don't deserve this. Your being late was unacceptable. Do you think that's any way to treat me? It's not okay to be late and to cancel on me like that. You're lucky I even agreed to see you today. Now crawl on your hands and knees." I lead him along the floor, not caring about any obstacles he may encounter. I savor the view of his ass as he crawls in front of me and can feel myself getting wet as I watch him. I know I'm pushing him, and myself, but I think both of us deserve a little added excitement.

He makes his way into the bedroom and heads towards the bed. I let him, but he's not going to climb into it as he might have had in mind. "Just stay right there," I bark at him as he approaches the edge of the bed. "I mean it, stay."

I walk around him, circling his body, inspecting it with care but trying to look aloof. He doesn't need to know how wet I am, at least not yet. I'm torn between looking at his sweet ass in the air and having him meet some other needs of mine. I bring the heel of my shoe down onto his asscheek and give a little kick. I can feel my breathing get heavier the minute my sole connects with him.

"So do you at least have an excuse? Or did you just think it was okay to be so disorganized that you'd be late and I wouldn't mind, without even a phone call? Huh?"

I poke at his ass a little more, deciding what else I'll dish out.

He looks up at me, his face contrite and childlike, and I almost give in, bring him into my lap for some cuddling. But then I remember the two long hours of waiting for him to arrive, my annoyance at having gotten painstakingly dressed up.

"Oh, no, you don't, don't even start with giving me those puppy-dog eyes. It's not going to work. In fact, it's just going to make me more angry. Get up."

I almost tell him to lie across my lap, but he doesn't deserve that kind of contact tonight. "Lean over the bed and spread your legs." I pick out the handcuffs we've used dozens of times to bind his wrists around each other.

I bring my hand up and smack him hard on the ass, watching his skin jiggle and redden at my touch. A shiver rushes through me at the motion, and I do it again. I look at his face, eyes closed in rapture even as he winces slightly; he wants it but doesn't want to want it. Plus, I've never been this genuinely angry with him before, we've never mixed real emotions with play in such a way, and it's exhilarating for me. I get to not just tell but show him exactly how pissed off I am. My next smack is harder than the others, and I stop pausing in between. Smack, smack, smack, smack! Hard enough to leave my hand stinging and make a sound that reverberates across the room. I feel another flush of arousal go through me and center in my cunt. I keep on spanking him, alternating cheeks and playing with my rhythm lest he get too used to it. He doesn't speak but his breaths came heavier and heavier, until they are almost, but not quite, groans. He doesn't want to give me the satisfaction of knowing how much he gets off on this, but I know, I can tell from the way his ass inches towards me in the tiniest of movements, the way his entire body forms a posture of submission. I reach again for the riding crop, lashing it against him in short, sharp strokes, firm. I feel like a machine, watching my hand rise and fall, the crop's tip making stealthy red welts, evidence of his poor manners.

I pause and rub my hand against his hot skin, smiling at its warmth. Both of us are playing a game, neither wanting the other to know just how much we not just like this, but need this, pretending aloofness or protest, but as I caress his ass, I tell him, with the soft touch of my hand, that he is not just forgiven, but loved. My hand moves slowly, a finger teasing his asshole, a hand trailing over his weighty ripe balls, to his cock, hard and eager and warm. I wrap my hand around it and hold it there for a moment, savoring the feel of having his precious arousal entirely within my grasp.

My mouth opens of its own volition as I stroke him, telling me beyond a shadow of a doubt how the rest of our evening is going to be spent. I draw him down onto the carpet with me, rolling him onto his back and kneeling before him. I look up at him, feel his eyes on me, questioning, and I nod. He knows this means that he has taken his punishment and he is forgiven, at least for the moment. While he's watching me, I bring my tongue out and trace a line around my lips, slowly and surely. His cock twitches in anticipation.

My eyes still on him, I lean down and lick a long, slow stroke of my tongue from the base of his cock to the head. I want his eyes on me, on us, while I perform this most intimate of sex acts. I open my mouth and slowly slide his hardness inside. This won't be some fast, sloppy, screaming blowjob. Not that I don't like giving those too, but this is different, special. While his cock is heavy in my mouth, in my power, my warmth and wetness surrounding him, coaxing him, we are communing on the deepest level possible. As the head of his cock presses against the roof of my mouth, then the farthest reaches of my throat, as I guide it through my taste buds, I savor every inch of flesh, every message imparted as our bodies connect. I slide him out of me, saliva oozing down my cheek, and rub his cock against my cheek, tenderly and reverently. I could do this all night, and all day, forever, really, if that were possible.

Instead I make the most of these fleeting moments, concentrating only on my mouth, the rest of me seeming to disappear. Just as he needed to be punished, to be beaten and face my wrath, I need this communion, the blessing of his cock as it plunges and plunders my mouth, finally releasing its hot nectar. I swallow, not wanting the magic of this moment to end, but knowing that it really doesn't have to. There'll be a next time, and a time after that, another chance to do all the things that I do best, to be cold and then hot, to bestow punishment and worship, anger and love. Much as he tries, my lover isn't known for his punctuality. Lucky for me, and for him.

Steam
by Deborah Kelly

I don't regularly visit my gym, although I did purchase a year-long membership in a burst of guilt last New Year's. I guess I thought that buying it would assuage me of my remorse for not being in better shape. In L.A., everyone is in better shape. Better shape than me, than my friends, than the airbrushed beauties in the smut magazines.

L.A. is filled with gorgeous people. All of them attend my gym.

Wrapped in sweats from head to toe, I walk, with my eyes down, to the treadmill. I could walk outside, I know. I could forgo this humiliating experience of striding through a room of thong-wearing, spandex-clad Barbie dolls. But then, I'd probably end up at the donut store and cancel out the effects of exercise. This way, at least I'll be forced to sweat. To pay for my latest chocolate spree.

I don't look at anyone while I jog in place. I look at a spot directly in front of the machine, fixate on it until I am practically mediating. This is why I don't notice the woman at my side waiting impatiently for me to finish. It's not until she says, rather rudely, "You've been on that for over thirty minutes. That's the max when someone's waiting," that I turn to look at her, nearly losing my balance in the process.

She is my age, early thirties. She has straw-colored hair swept from her lovely face in a ponytail and she looks like an actress I've seen on one of the soaps. I look closer as I press the "stop" button on my machine, realizing she *is* the actress I've seen. Of course, she is. All of the actresses you've seen have memberships at my gym.

I murmur an apology for keeping her waiting, then shuffle to one of the racks of weights and start lifting. Again, I lose myself, but this time I am meditating on her, visualizing myself as I peel off her red spandex tights, cut through her black spandex thong, wrap the spandex straps around her wrists to capture her.

I have her tied and tormented before I realize that she's staring at me in the mirror. I look at my own reflection rather than meeting her gaze. I am wearing black sweats in a sea of colored spandex. My corkscrew ringlets are free and curling wilder than ever because I'm hot and sweaty. My normally pale cheeks have circles of color, "apples of color" my grandmother would say, in their centers.

I'm not overweight. I'm not even untoned. I simply do not look like the Malibu girls who grace the Stairmaster machines. I do not have a swishy ponytail nor a face you've seen on TV. I don't have to. I work behind the camera.

When I'm done with my self-scrutiny, I realize she's still watching me. *Whatever*, I think, mimicking my hairdresser who accentuates the statement by making a little "w" with his fingers and thumbs. Then, because I am uncomfortable, I head to the showers, and then to the steam room.

That's where she finds me. She comes in, wearing only a towel, but holding her leotard in one hand. She says, "You were looking at me in the oddest way," which is funny, because this is exactly what I want to say to her. She says, " I don't think we'll be interrupted. There's a step class going on and all the women are in there, sweating."

I say, "But we're in here, sweating..." and she drops her towel and lets me ogle her beautiful form for a moment before coming toward me and offering me that twisted rope of red lycra. I don't hesitate. I let her lay down on the white towel on top of the wood boards while I wrap her leotard around her wrists. I don't have the rest of the accoutrements to trick out my envisioned torture chamber, but I like the way she looks as is. Bound, semi-helpless, her muscular thighs spread, her body arched and ready.

I climb up next to her on the wood bench and I part those sturdy thighs and go instantly to work. She's wet from her post-workout shower, but she's also wet from want, and the subtle flavor of her cunt envelopes me in the same manner as the steam does. It goes to my head, but it's too tasty to pull away from. I lose myself in her cunt. I would climb inside her if I could. I know I should practice a bit of foreplay, let her see what a dutiful and passionate lover I can be. Instead, I go for the prize in the box of Crackerjacks, fastening my lips in a circle around her clitoris and sucking on it as if it were a piece of hard candy, an everlasting gobstopper that gets sweeter as it melts in your mouth.

She moans and tries to use her hands to push me down on her, but they're tied and helpless. That spurs me on and I lift her thighs up over my shoulders and impale her asshole with my fingers, never moving my lips from her cunt. She's still as I probe her insides, she's completely still, as if I might stop if she moves. I can see how much she likes it, likes the feeling of intrusion there, and that makes me wish I had a dildo to impale her with, instead of only my fingers.

We're both sweating wildly now, but she's close to coming and I bring her to the very peak with fingers, tongue, mouth, the palm of my free hand on her ass, the dig of my nails into her skin. I know the step class must be nearly over, that I need to finish this up and so I keep my busy fingers in her ass, my hungry mouth sealed to her pussy. Her orgasm is an explosion of juices all over my face and lips and sticky fingers. We're both wrecked as we hear the door open and we quickly hide beneath our towels, her with her bound wrists hidden.

We share secret smiles on the way back to the showers, and she says, "I'm glad I skipped 'step workout' today."

I cock my head at her, and bite my tongue, thinking to myself, "Heck, if it burns up the calories, who's to complain?"

Here, In the Middle of Everything
by John Flores

At your request, I drive us to The Hollywood Bowl, a concert hall that's built in the basin scooped out of a hill, where we can listen to the music of the yearly jazz festival. It's a tradition of ours. But the tradition includes much more than simply enjoying the melodious jazz. You've bought seats at the top of the bleachers, where nobody pays patrons any attention: the cheap seats. Perfect for our annual outdoor festivities.

We park at the base of the hill and walk up, carrying our picnic basket and blanket. After giving our tickets to the usher, we take several escalators to the very top of the Bowl. The bleacher seats up here are nearly empty. Most people have crowded down low, to watch the musicians play. You and I have ulterior motives. We want a little privacy, and we can hear the music fine even way up here. For us, the music is simply a backdrop to our own enchanted pleasures.

Once we spread out, I help you lay down in my lap, so that you're truly comfortable. Your feet are up on the wood and your eyes are closed. I stroke your shiny hair away from your forehead and look down at your pretty face as the musicians continue to play.

It looks as if there are fireflies in the sky, but I know that heralding lights are simply picking up the white wings of moths high up in the air. Still, the scene is plenty atmospheric, and when I bend down to kiss you, I feel you squirm against my lap. You're letting me know what I know already. I'm hard. But now, from the way you're moving, I sense you're trying to tell me something. You want to do something about my hardness.

Here, in the middle of everything.

I wrap us even tighter in the quilt, and then feel your body as you move down, on your knees, still fully hidden by the blanket. I sigh as your hands fumble in hazy darkness for my fly. You unbutton the row of faded gold buttons with a quick tug, and then almost instantly your mouth is on me. Warm and soft and sweet.

I have nothing on under the jeans, and with the fly parted open, you can bob up and down almost all the way to the base. The feeling is unbelievable. Yeah, we play oral games at home, whenever we want to, but being out in public is different. Being so well cared for while among thousands of other people is almost surreal. I can't get enough of the sensation. It's the fact that we are here, in the middle of everything, doing this most base and private act that makes me want to shoot right now. But I force myself to stay steady, to hold the course, to not rush.

Breathing in deep, I close my eyes, then open them a second later as I feel your fingertips pushing beneath me to stroke my balls through my jeans. I'm not sure how much of this I can take. But you don't care. You seem to move to the very beat of the music, rocking your mouth with a rhythmic cadence, up and down, sucking in hard, and then relaxing. I feel myself getting dizzy, lightheaded from the way you move.

God, do you know how to suck cock.

You have these little special tricks that you do, swirls with your tongue, designs you seem to make as if you're trying to tell me something, or transform me into someone else. And you do. With your little moves and your special suckling kisses, you push me right over the edge, until I'm falling into the music and the pleasure of being so well treated. Falling and rising up again. No more waiting. No more holding back.

And as the music sways over me, I know that I'm going to come.

Here, in the middle of everything.

Stained
by Rhonda Lewis

I don't know how he knew that it was my time of the month, but he always did. Crazy, wasn't it? Most of my boyfriends have been extremely careful to avoid those five to seven days each month—or if not to avoid me, then to avoid my pussy in favor of my mouth for one-sided oral pleasures, or my ass for pleasures of a different type altogether.

But not Ed. Ed had a knack.

When I read back over my diary from the time we were together, I can tell that he knew precisely what he was doing. Yet at the time, I didn't have any idea. Why should I have? I was eighteen, a freshman in college, without a clue about the fetishes that make different people tick. He was twenty-one, a junior, and he knew exactly what he liked.

Some call it vampire sex. He never had a name for what turned him on. Never once spoke about the concept out loud. He only came by my room, cuddled up with me, held my hand or stroked my hair. And if my roommate left us alone for a moment, he'd pin me down on the long, thin twin mattress and kiss me, sweetly, firmly, until I felt myself start to respond. It wouldn't take much. I liked Ed, so when he started to tease me, I always felt my body answer his overtures.

But at some point, as his strong hands wandered to my plaid pajama bottoms, I'd realize that I'd have to tell him— "I can't tonight."

"Why?"

Soft shrug, embarrassed grin. A look in my eyes that begged him not to make me say it. I was shy. An eighteen-year-old sexual novice. I didn't have any of the necessary experiences to help me muddle through situations like this.

"Come on," he'd press. "Why, baby?"

"I've got my—"

But Ed would never let me finish the sentence. He'd silence my words with a well-timed kiss. And then we'd do it. Somewhere, anywhere. In my room, if Lisa were out of town or studying in the library. In his, if we could bribe his over-zealous roommate to go read his chemistry books out in the lounge. Ed didn't care about the mess, or the stains. He just wanted to fuck me, and his obvious want fueled my own desire. The way he looked at me with his hazel eyes, the way he touched me, stroked me, and talked to me, made me as turned on as he was.

And I still remember—

The feeling of being incredibly sexy without worries. The feeling of being wanted, without rules or barriers, without the need to be freshly showered and powdered dry. Since Ed, I've never been with a guy so in tune with my rhythms. Most of my men haven't wanted to broach that area, but he showed me that it didn't matter. The mess of it. The stickiness. He went deep and let everything happen. That was his fetish, the slight bit of kink that he liked, even though we never talked about it.

I'm more aware now. I can spot someone who needs a little something extra to get into the mood. Whether it's dressing up in frilly lingerie or playing with edible oils, using sex toys or viewing porn, I can easily read that yearning look in a lover's eye. I can spot the glazed gaze of someone who's addicted to some sort of kink. Any sort of kink. And, really, we all are on one level or another, aren't we?

But Ed had made peace with his. He knew that if he played me just right, I would melt into his embrace, liquify in his arms. I think I understand, now, too. I think I can picture what he liked about doing it during that particular time of the month, the baseness of the act. The natural flood of it. I was warmer and wetter. There was something ancient, animalistic, about the way we fucked.

When he moved to an apartment off campus, he still seemed to know the right time to call. "Come see a movie," he'd suggest. "My roommate's out for the night." And I'd drive the half-mile to his place and we'd sit on the sofa as if we really were going to catch a flick.

As if.

Within moments, he'd be on me, pushing me down. I'd run to the bathroom to get ready, and he'd call me back to him, fucking me on the brown shag rug, making such a mess that we had to move the sofa to cover the stains.

But he didn't care.

That's the part that I remember the most. He didn't care.

Just now, after reading through a chronicle of my freshman year in my battered old diary, I realize that every month, like clockwork, there he was. Ready and waiting to see the stains we could leave.

Debut
by Sasha Johnson

My lover, a director-to-be, staged a fabulous filming fiesta on Saturday. Screenwriter/director/producer/caterer (providing pizza and beer for all), she generously cast me as the star of her semi-autobiographical video.

I played her.

This taxed my already quite limited acting abilities to the max. Conveying a drop-dead redhead with Mediterranean blue eyes is difficult enough for a brown-on-brown girl, anyhow. But after three beers on an empty stomach (which might not fell your average movie star, but knocks this feather-weight down for the count) I sprouted a full-grown Hollywood ego. Soon our guests/co-stars began to wonder who died and made me Sean Young.

It's not an experience I'm proud of, and one I only (thankfully) remember vaguely.

What I do remember is watching Cassandra shoo our company out the front door, saying in her hushed, unhurried tone, "That's a wrap for today. We'll finish up next weekend."

Then I remember her stalking, seriously *stalking* over to me, her calm face changing completely as she made her way to my side. "You..." she began, sticking a finger in my face. "You need to deal with yourself."

I was puzzled, and drunk, and I said, "What do you mean?"

"Bossing people around like a Diva. What gives? Your job was to help me out. Becoming a prima donna is not in your contract."

I relaxed again on our sofa and opened another bottle, feeling no pain. She ended that, taking the Corona out of my hand and sitting down next to me.

"If you act spoiled, I will treat you like a spoiled child," she said, more to herself, than to me. I gave her another one of my puzzled looks, and was surprised even more as she pulled me over her lap and lifted my silver-spangled dress.

"This is not a game," she hissed, pulling my lace panties down my thighs. "This was a serious day of filming that you ruined."

I felt the smack of her hand on my naked ass before I truly realized what was going on. Then, in the whining tone she despises—I should have known better—I said, "But we goof around in front of the camera all the time." (This is true. We film dinner parties, park picnics, ourselves in bed... everything.)

"This is my senior project," she yelled, punctuating each word with another blow to my naked ass, making me squirm and try to get away. She held me firmly in place. "I need this film to be good," she said, softer now, almost lost beneath the resounding smacks of her hand punishing my ass. I looked at our reflection in the mirror across the room. My bum was a deep, cherry red and by the look on Cassandra's face, it was going to be magenta before she finished. I decided to do some apologizing. Quickly.

"Really," I slurred, trying to push up so I could talk to her. A firm hand pressed me back on the sofa. "I was just messing around."

Her hand moved lower to heat the backs of my thighs. I howled and squirmed more, but she would not let up.

"I'll be good next week," I said next, "I promise." She didn't stop.

My mind raced with possible explanations for my behavior. When I realized that I couldn't come up with anything in my defense, I stilled myself and accepted her wrath. I'd earned it.

Finally, when a stream of tears had covered my cheeks, Cassie shoved me off her lap and glared down at me.

"At least we got one good take," she said, sounding more like herself. Calm. Easy.

I pulled my panties up and straightened my dress. "What do you mean," I asked, much quieter now, completely cowed. She pointed in the direction of her camera, still on the tripod, still running. I felt my face go pale.

"We'll start with that next weekend," she said. "I'm sure the crew will be thrilled."

I stared at my hands, and in a low, humble voice, I said, "Cassie. I'm sorry."

She sat on the floor at my side and took me in her arms, as she always does when I've gone through a punishment session. "I know you are," she said. "It's over now. And we'll keep that tape for a reminder...."

Then she led me into the bedroom, where our second camera is set up on permanent display, and we made another, different kind of movie.

Teacher's Pet
by Naomi Vanderbilt

"Practice makes perfect. You know that, Angie. C'mon girl, give it a bit more, won't you?"

I struggled through the text, stumbling over the pronunciation of two words that I didn't recognize, trying so hard to grasp the poet's meaning, all the while aware of Mr. Bradshaw pacing behind me, rapping his ruler against the palm of his hand for emphasis. If I looked toward the window, I could see his reflection, a shimmering hazy figure as he walked back and forth, over to the velvet fainting couch along the far wall, and then returning, in a looping route, by the piano, around the antique coffee table, and ending behind my high-backed chair.

"Once more," he said when I'd finished the passage. "Your accent is off, and it doesn't sound as if you're really concentrating. Do it again."

The tears began to well up in my eyes when I found my mind refusing to cooperate, my tongue clumsy, my lips thick, trying to waltz around the foreign words, but skipping, falling, failing him. Again.

He stood just to the side of my chair, that ruler smacking his palm over and over, a mindless, random habit. A metronome, reminding me of punishments past and punishments present.

"Please, Sir." I whispered, so afraid of saying the wrong thing, but not able to continue with the poem, not able to make my mind stretch to encompass the meaning of the words. "Please can we stop for today."

I was aware of the fact that he'd be disappointed. I knew I'd be disciplined. But Baudelaire in English is difficult enough for me to understand and the French can be even more problematical.

When Mr. Bradshaw sat on the lounge and faced me, motioning to me, I knew what was coming. I stood and quickly came to his side, then to avoid making it worse on myself, pulled up my skirt and bent over his lap. The ruler was no stranger to my ass. I have been under the tutelage of Mr. Bradshaw for three years, since my eighteenth birthday, and that ruler knows exactly where the most tender spots are located. The plump underside of my asscheeks, the backs of my thighs.

Failing in my lessons is good for ten blows, usually. Today, the third day we'd fought with the same poem, he meted out twenty, insisting I count each one for him. It's not an easy task to do through choked, harsh sobs. He gave me three at once, then touched each one as I said, "One, two, three..." in a halting, humble voice. Then he repeated those same strokes, in the same places, as if for emphasis, and by "six," my face was drenched with tears.

Mr. Bradshaw's job is to teach me decorum and etiquette as well as serving as my private tutor. I mustn't squirm over his lap when he punishes me. I must stay still and take what I deserve. I know this to be so, but I cannot comprehend how to follow the rules. I rock on his lap, pressing my hips against his legs, attempting to reduce the pain by sparking that warm feeling of pleasure between my thighs.

It's bad, I know. But I can't help myself. I'm weak. When he finishes, when he pushes me off his lap and tells me to be more prepared tomorrow, I will retreat to my room, seat myself on my canopied bed, and rub with two fingers around and around my clit. I will imagine that it is him, my teacher, bringing me such sinful pleasures. I will pretend that he catches me in the act, that he climbs onto my bed and finishes the job for me with his tongue, before punishing me even more severely for my transgressions, for my lack of willpower.

It's all mixed up in my mind. Pain, pleasure, pain, pleasure, like the slapping sound of his ruler on his palm. That's what throws me, that noise. It makes me wet, makes me unable to concentrate, and I break down, do the wrong thing, and get what I want.

He demands that I count now, raising the blows to twenty-five because I was unable to stay still. Then he pushes me off, looking down at me with that strange mixture of disappointment and... and... what?

He says, "Angie, go to your room. I expect you to be more prepared tomorrow." As I lower my skirts and adjust my petticoats, he says, "Now go upstairs... and wait for me."

And this time, as I leave the room in my hurried pace, there is a smile on my face beneath the tears.

More than a Mouthful
by Michael Bell

You know how some women stress out about the size of their breasts? If you're a woman, I'm sure you know all about it. If you don't worry, your friends probably do. For some reason, there's this obsession with big tits. I don't know if it's an American thing, or it happens everywhere. Red-blooded American men are supposed to be into breasts the size of cantaloupes—D-cup at least, preferably double-D or triple-D. Sometimes it seems like sex is all about cleavage.

Make whatever assumption you want to about me—I'm into small ones.

That's why it turns me on so much to be with Lisa.

Twenty-six and auburn-haired, Lisa's as slender as a gymnast even though she prefers to kick-box. She's too big for an A-cup, but not quite big enough for a B. She calls them "A+." I prefer the term "A++." I've had girls with A+ tits before, and these are definitely better. Just a hint fuller, with big, firm nipples and *almost*—but not quite—enough weight to suspend a pencil under them. That's the classic test of whether a girl needs a bra, and my own particular upward limit of what absolutely drives me wild. In fact, I think it's perfect. If I could spend the rest of my life making love to Lisa's tits, I would die a happy man. In fact, I would probably starve to death with my mouth on Lisa's nipples, unaware of the wasting of my body. And I would still be the happiest man on earth.

Am I objectifying her? Probably. But Lisa doesn't seem to mind.

The first time we were together, I couldn't take my hands, my mouth, my face off of those gorgeous tits of hers. I couldn't believe how perfect they were—the pair of tits I had dreamed about my entire life. I was surprised that she wore a bra—she didn't really need one. She would later confess that she'd worn a bra because she didn't want me to think she was a slut—and, I discovered, because it was one of those bust enhancement bras with firm padding underneath, lifting and separating her breasts into an approximation of cleavage. She confessed to me a week later that she'd been quite sure I wouldn't want to sleep with her if she didn't have at least a little more than a mouthful.

In fact, when I eased her top off and unhitched the front clasp of her Wonderbra, Lisa blushed a little and asked me if I minded that they were too small. She was embarrassed to ask it, and covered up her shyness by giggling that some guys thought anything more than a mouthful was wasted.

I responded by spending long hours making love to them, discovering that Lisa could come without ever having me enter her or touch her clit. Some girls can, you see. It just takes a really, really long time. Which doesn't bother me even a little bit.

Lisa eventually confessed to me that she loves her breasts touched, that she never, ever gets tired of it. But that night, she didn't say a word; she just let me do exactly what I wanted to do, and while she was moaning in rapture and thinking she was being too indulgent, I was doing exactly the same thing. In her mind, she was thanking God over and over again that I was being so considerate as to lavish tons of affection on her "too-small" breasts; I, similarly, was almost weeping with joy as I thanked my lucky stars that I'd found a small-busted girl willing to indulge my selfish need to make love to her tits all night.

I even kept touching them when I ate her out, that night, which I did for so long my jaw ached and Lisa told me she didn't think she could come again (she proved herself wrong). As my tongue explored her pussy, sliding deep between her lips and teasing her clit, my hands were upthrust, my fingertips caressing her little mounds, my thumbs and forefingers pinching her nipples, her hands clutched hard on mine and encouraging me to keep stroking her firm tits.

When she came again, the third time, I still couldn't stop. I tried to, because I told myself I should let this poor girl get some sleep. But when she cradled my head against her chest, I was on them again—uncontrolled, weak-willed, so hungry for them that I couldn't stop. My hands, my mouth, my face and my cock were all over them. I was the happiest man alive.

I could have shot my load just from touching them, but I didn't—because I couldn't bear the idea that I might get sleepy afterwards, and not be able to keep doing what I was doing.

They weren't really more than a mouthful. But then, I've only got one mouth.

That first night together, when the sun came up and I was still caressing Lisa's breasts, licking them, sucking them, rubbing her hard nipples, now pink and puffy with wear, against my cheek, savoring the feel, my new lover asked me: "Don't you want to fuck?"

"I would love to fuck," I sighed, kissing her as my hands roved over her breasts. "But I'm also totally happy to do this for another twenty-four hours."

She looked at the clock. Six a.m. on a Sunday.

"We've got twenty-seven," she sighed, and pushed my head back down between her tits. "Make them count."

And I did—just as I've made every hour in bed with Lisa count, ever since.

Veronica's Lover
by N.T. Morley

Veronica's lover had tied her to the bed face-up with leather restraints around her wrists and ankles, leaving just enough give in the ropes lashed to the head- and footboard so that Veronica could struggle deliciously. Veronica was blinded with a padded leather blindfold padlocked around her head, but she was not gagged.

"Anything," Veronica had told her lover. "Anything at all. You can do anything to me."

Which might have been a dangerous request for her birthday, if Veronica hadn't allowed her lover to read her diary. Veronica's diary was not like most other diaries; instead, it was a many-volumed collection of erotic fantasies, ranging from the sublime to the extreme. She knew, because she knew her lover so well, that tonight, on her birthday, she would be forced—"forced" was the word that excited her when she was tied up like this, though she wanted nothing more than to *be* forced, making it a strange word to use—she would be forced to experience one of those fantasies. But which one? One of her fondest, a fantasy that she had written and rewritten in a dozen incarnations throughout the hundreds of pages tucked into her loose-leaf binder? Or one of the scary ones, a fantasy she had written in a moment of audacious extremity and forgotten about entirely, one that would terrify and excite her as she groped in her memory for every detail she had written down?

Her breath came fast as she heard the bedroom door opening and closing.

She heard soft footsteps approaching the bed, took a deep breath and smelled a body, unfamiliar—a stranger. Perfume, just a hint of it, mingled with the scent of sex, her own and the stranger's. She felt the weight on the bed and her body tensed as smooth fingers ran up her body, touching first her thighs, then her wet pussy, making her gasp and squirm as she felt herself penetrated, invaded, as she felt her clit teased. Then the hand, now moist with Veronica's juices, trailed its way up Veronica's belly and over her breasts, pinching her nipples, squeezing her breasts—then, quite unexpectedly, traveling to Veronica's face so the fingers, slick with pussy, could be forced between Veronica's parted lips.

She licked, savoring her own juices. She felt a hot mouth on one nipple, suckling it, making it stiffen more as her pussy responded with pulses that matched the strokes of the stranger's tongue.

When the hand and mouth left her, Veronica longed for them back. A mouth pressed to hers, tasting different than her lover's, different than any mouth she'd ever tasted. She felt a tongue, long and lithe, pressing its way into her mouth, opening her up, preparing her. Then Veronica felt the weight shifting atop her, the stranger changing position, her knees tucked alongside Veronica's upper torso, calves underneath Veronica's upper arms. Smooth thighs surrounded Veronica's face, caressing her cheeks as the stranger's crotch made its way down onto Veronica's face.

She smelled it, sharp and tangy. Sex. Female sex. She felt it, against her mouth, wriggling, descending as the thighs pressed tighter against her, forcing this stranger's pussy against Veronica's open mouth, stifling her panting moans with the inexorable press of moist folds of flesh.

Veronica felt a surge of arousal go through her nude body as her tongue found the strange woman's entrance. The taste was so unfamiliar to her, so new and exotic. Hungrily, she began to feed, her tongue licking from the woman's smooth, slick opening to the firm bud of her clit, listening to the faint moans of ecstasy as she began to work the woman's clit. She had mounted the bed with her ass toward Veronica, and as Veronica lapped at the woman's pussy she felt an unfamiliar mouth on her own cunt, so helpless and vulnerable between her open thighs. Veronica's moans were muffled by the strange woman's pussy as she felt a tongue working its way between her lips. As she felt the tip of that tongue pressing her clit.

Veronica felt the electric charge exploding through her, her arousal mounting as her ass lifted off the bed. The woman was larger than her, and her weight bore Veronica into the bed. Veronica ate her pussy hungrily as the woman ground her hips rhythmically in time with Veronica's ministrations. Meanwhile, the woman found the perfect rhythm on Veronica's cunt, and Veronica sank desperately into pleasure, giving herself over to it.

Was Veronica's lover watching her? Standing in the doorway savoring Veronica's surrender? Had her lover trained a video camera on her, to capture this moment for later enjoyment? Or was this moment Veronica's alone—Veronica's, and the stranger's?

Slender fingers worked their way into Veronica's pussy; she gasped as their soft pads hit her G-spot firmly and began to massage it. Veronica squirmed against the bonds, each movement of her body accenting both the suckling hunger of her mouth and the press of the strange woman's tongue on her clit—not to mention the rush of unexpected pleasure deep in her pussy. Veronica was going to come. She knew it. But she wanted this woman to come, too; she wanted to pleasure the stranger as much as the stranger was pleasuring her.

To her surprise, as Veronica licked harder, suckling on the woman's clit, the fingers left her and the pussy-slick hands gripped her thighs, as the strange woman's hips began to buck and pump. Veronica licked faster, not letting up until the woman had shuddered and climaxed on top of her, moaning uncontrollably with each stroke of Veronica's tongue.

Then, with a gasp, she lifted her pussy off of Veronica's face, as if unable to bear any more stimulation. Veronica's mouth still worked involuntarily, her tongue lolling out to lick after the pussy denied her. Then, her mouth went slack as she felt the fingers pushing into her again, as she felt the mouth descending on her pussy again. As she felt the tongue on her clit and her entire body exploded in sensation.

It took moments, this time; the feel and sound and smell and taste of the woman climaxing on top of her had driven Veronica over the edge. In the moments before her orgasm, she wondered again if her lover was watching, if her lover had arranged to savor this moment later—or if this orgasm, this intense climax that was about to explode through her, was hers alone—hers and the stranger's.

Veronica felt her muscles spasming, the first hint that she was coming. Then, a split-second later, the pleasure burst through her naked, bound body and she let out an unrestrained wail of ecstasy, her whole body shaking as she released herself into the stranger's touch. She felt the room spinning, unseen, as she lost herself in the sensations and bright lights exploded in her eyes behind the blindfold.

Still whimpering, Veronica felt the strange woman licking her pussy clean, devouring the juices that had leaked onto her thighs. When she felt the woman rising, Veronica took a great sobbing breath and felt the cold of the room hit her, the woman's body heat vanished in an instant. She wanted to lift her head and look—to see if her lover was there—but she could see only blackness, the smooth inky blackness of the leather blindfold.

Veronica heard footsteps. Two sets of them. One, getting further away.

One set of footsteps, coming closer.

She heard the door open, pause in silence, and close.

She took a deep breath, smelled the familiar scent. She felt her lips parting in a rapturous smile, heard herself whispering her lover's name.

Heard the greeting returned, "Veronica" whispered, soft and close. Tasted the familiar kiss on her lips.

Veronica felt the weight as her mounted the bed, heard the bed creak as she strained upward against the bonds, wanting to savor the weight atop her. That weight bore her into the bed, and Veronica surrendered to it.

Battery Power
by Thomas S. Roche

"Oh, *fuck*," she said. "How am I going to get this report done?"

"How about your laptop?" I asked.

"It's not charged." I watched Quinn pout, illuminated in pizzicato by the apocalyptic flashes of lightning coming through the rain-dappled window.

I shrugged in the dark, a strange feeling. "I'll get the candles," I said.

I went into the kitchen to get a flashlight, and the battery-powered radio. I also nabbed a half-drunk bottle of Merlot. I went into the bedroom for the candles...and picked up something else, just in case. When I returned, Quinn had moved her pouting to the sofa. The lightning flashed and my heart went out to her—she looked really miserable. She was so miserable she didn't even notice the wine.

"I just hope the power's not out long," she said. "I *have* to finish this fucking report."

I set the radio down and turned it on.

"....knocked out power lines, leaving more than 20,000 residents without power. The storm also..."

"That was quick," she said.

I went around the room lighting candles. She leaned over and flipped the dial.

"....knocked down power lines, stranding..."

"....major power outages...."

I sat on the sofa next to her, close.

"....for all you lovers stranded in candlelight out there, this is a little tune that should put you in the mood."

The strains of "Let's Get It On" floated through the lightning-strobed darkness. Quinn's hand paused on the dial. She looked at me suspiciously, her eyes narrowing.

I uncorked the wine and took a sip straight from the bottle.

"We're out of clean glasses," I said. "I'll run the dishwasher as soon as the power comes back on. Are you finished complaining or do you still need to be pissed off for a while?"

She looked at me with her lips pursed. I smiled, offering her the bottle.

She took her hand off the dial of the radio.

She needed a drink even more than I did. When her lips came off the bottle, I pressed mine to them, tasting the spicy red wine and putting my arms around her. I expected her to protest, but she melted right into me. Marvin Gaye was telling us to fuck, and who's going to argue with a sexual icon?

Her tongue was warm and sharp from the wine. I took the bottle from her and had another sip, then set the bottle on the end table, which provided me a convenient excuse to lean over, pushing Quinn into a prone position. She didn't protest; on the contrary, she hugged me tight and murmured softly.

I pulled up her T-shirt and began to kiss my way across her breasts. When I reached one nipple I suckled it gently into my mouth and Quinn's legs spread smoothly around my hips, drawing me deeper into her embrace. She felt the lump in my back pocket and nudged it with her toe.

"What's that?"

"I'll give you a hint," I said. "It's battery powered."

Quinn sighed faintly, kissing the top of my head.

I moved to her other nipple and she arched her back, moaning tenderly, running her fingers through my hair. I ground my body against hers, and when she felt the firmness of my cock pushing through my jeans, she lifted her ass slightly, pushing back against me. As I suckled her tits, I slipped her shirt over her head and tossed it on the ground. I slipped my hands under the waistband of her sweats and eased them down her body. She slid one leg out of them and I eased down, spreading her legs further, lifting her thighs up into the air as I knelt in front of the sofa.

Lightning flashed all over us, mingling with the flickering candlelight to illuminate Quinn's pretty face. Her lips parted wide and she moaned as my tongue teased her clit. I slid two fingers into her and she gripped the sofa, shuddering. I licked faster, harder, my free hand traveling up to tease her nipples, my palms opening to stroke the firm buds. Quinn grasped my hand and pushed it hard against her breast, then drew it up to suckle on my fingers as I felt her clit swelling still more under my tongue.

Marvin Gaye had stopped telling us to fuck, but now that chick from the Divinyls was crooning about touching herself, and Quinn saw no reason to stop taking the radio's advice. Her hand slid down to her clit and she started rubbing it as I licked down around her lips, teasing them open so I could slide my hand in more firmly. When I returned to her clit, my tongue pressed harder against it and Quinn uttered a choking gasp of pleasure, both hands now grasping mine. She lost interest in my fingers and shoved the heel of my hand into her mouth, biting hard as I drove her closer. I reached into the back of my sweats and took out my secret weapon—a slim, battery-powered vibrator. When I pressed it to her clit, Quinn went crazy.

"Fuck, fuck, fuck, fuck, fuck," she moaned. Quinn squeezed the muscles of her pussy around my fingers as I pushed up and stroked her G-spot. Her moans rose in intensity. I could tell she was right on the edge, and it was that critical moment when I decided whether to get her off with my tongue and my hands, or fuck the living daylights out of her.

Quinn solved that dilemma: "Fuck me," she moaned. "I want to come with you inside me."

I turned off the vibrator, shucked my sweats and pushed Quinn back onto the sofa. She spread her legs and closed them around me, grabbing my hair and pushing my mouth against hers. I entered her in an easy stroke, her pussy warm around my cock. I started fucking her slowly, and then it happened. The lights went on all around us, and the stereo, which had been playing the modern rock-industrial-metal station, blazed into surging noise, mingling with the sexy strains of love songs from the battery-powered radio. White Zombie drowned out Barry White and the blaze of lights washed over our trysting bodies as Quinn's computer made that musical sound that meant it was time to start work. But she wasn't listening. Her body pumped against mine, naked and spread on the couch, her fingernails digging into me as she clawed and moaned. I slid the vibrator down between us and touched it to Quinn's clit as I fucked her—and in an instant, she came, her eyes going wide in unexpected ecstasy and release, her arms and legs seizing me and pulling me hard onto her so I lost hold of the vibrator. The tight press of our bodies wedged it even harder against Quinn's clit, and she writhed as her orgasm intensified.

The pumping of my hips drove my cock into her rhythmically, and when I came, Quinn whispered "Come inside me" and nuzzled my ear as I did. The noisy strains of two kinds of music were all drowned out as Quinn's computer surged into AutoPlay, its tinny speakers blasting the Ramones CD in her DVD-ROM drive. Everything pulsed over us—lights, music, orgasms. The lightning and thunder were all lost in the melee. I sank down on top of her and sighed against her flesh. Quinn reached down and turned off the vibrator, tossing it onto the coffee table.

"Want to get back to work?" I asked her. "I mean, the power's back on." I had to talk loud for her to hear me over the blaring strains of music.

She curled her arms tighter and wrapped herself around me.

"Maybe that report can wait until tomorrow, after all," she said.

Whole
by Kinde Moore

He fucked my ass last night. It's not the first time we've done it, but it's the first time I liked it. More than that. It's the first time I asked him to do it, begged him to do it.

"Please, Hunter, please..."

We fuck raw. We fuck like animals. Hard, heavy, the sweat-sheen gleaming on our bodies. We fit together like pieces of a puzzle, two strikingly similar bodies, long, lean, muscular. When I look at our reflection in the mirror, sometimes it's like seeing double. Often when we're out, people ask if we're related.

Now *there's* a twisted thought.

When we fuck, Hunter puts the mirror right next to the bed so that we can watch. He likes to watch. It's one of his favorite things. He says, "See, that's you. That's the way you look when I'm inside you."

I stare at my reflection, seeing but not seeing. Falling into myself, into the hot gold glow of my brown eyes, the parted-helpless look of my lips. I look hungry when we fuck. I look overwhelmed.

Last night, though, was different.

He said, "Touch yourself. Find that clit of yours and stroke it."

Fingers wet, clumsy, finding the hard nub of tingling flesh and rubbing, rubbing, rubbing.

He said, "Watch while you come. Watch your face change."

I wasn't close to coming. I was on fire. My skin burned. I wanted something more. I tugged at my clit, rubbed it hard with my third finger, knowing I'd be sore the next day, but not caring. I looked into my eyes, as he wanted me to do. Then I looked into his eyes and I said, "Please, Hunter, please...."

"Please what?" His cock was stroking me inside, pushing against the walls of my cunt, touching me in all the places that usually work to get me off but weren't working last night. "Please what?"

"Put it in my ass." It was difficult for me to say, and I looked down at the bed when the words were out of my mouth. He reached forward, cupped my chin in his hand and forced my head up.

"Look at yourself," he demanded.

I did.

"Now, say it again."

I bit my bottom lip, not wanting to obey. I kept my fingers going, making those endless rotations that only I know how to make. I said, "Please, Hunt. Please..." My voice got hoarse and lowered in pitch. "Please put it in my ass."

"Put *what* in your ass?"

My head wanted to go down again. My eyes wanted to focus on the bed, on the pillows, on anything but my reflection. He wouldn't let me.

"Put your cock in my ass," I said, in a rush, all at once to get it out.

"Why?"

He pulled it from my cunt and moved away as he asked, and being emptied of him was a horrifying sensation. I needed his touch. I needed his body against mine.

"I want..." I started, unsure, "I want to feel it."

"You want to feel it deep inside you—" His cock was already wet with my cunt juices and he parted the cheeks of my ass and pressed the head of it against my hole.

I nodded, keeping my eyes on his in the mirror as he bucked his hips forward and drove the thing home.

And I liked it. I liked the fullness of it. The weight of it inside me. It was different than the other times, when he's taken me by force. It was a partnership and I moved back on him and used my body with his and relaxed against him.

Sometimes when I stare at my reflection, I look overwhelmed. Last night was different. Last night, I looked satiated. I looked complete.

I looked whole.

Topless

by Peter Lieberman

Bridget lets me choose her clothes. I look at her in everything she wears, making sure it's sexy enough to satisfy me. And sexy enough to satisfy her.

This outfit, however, I've never seen on her before, not really. At least, not the way it's intended to be worn. Even though I picked it out. Even though she tried it on for me. Even though I'd paid for it with my credit card when she'd balked at the price.

I wanted her close as possible to naked.

Bridget's a little shy. More than a little, actually. She's also a shameless exhibitionist. It doesn't sound like those two traits can go together? Well, they can—in fact, they're deliciously adapted for each other.

My beautiful girlfriend is embarrassed about the fact that men look at her; even more embarrassed about the fact that she *wants* men to look at her. That it makes her wet. That's why she lets me pick out her clothes. Because nothing makes me hotter than knowing every guy who lays eyes on Bridget is eating his heart out, wanting her.

Bridget's a little uncomfortable with her large, full breasts, her slender belly, the smooth swell of her hips. She's a little uncomfortable with her long, glorious legs, and with the fact that just by showing them off as she walks down the street she can have a man tripping on his tongue, running his car into a fire hydrant, wishing to God he could have those legs wrapped around his face.

If it wasn't for me, Bridget would wear loose sweats, baggy jeans, bulky sweaters. And spend her whole life longing to show off. With me, she gets to show off all she wants, and even if she feels a little nervous about it, even if she says "I can't" or "Don't make me" the first time, she gets to do it anyway. She gets to be shameless—and I never push her past the boundaries of "tasteful."

Well, *almost* never.

Because the outfit she's wearing now, it's anything but tasteful. When she tried it on for me, she had on a pair of cotton underwear beneath the spandex sliver of fabric, in accordance with state health laws.

"If you make me buy this," she whispered into my ear, her face hot against mine as she blushed, "I'll have to get a Brazilian wax."

"That's right," I told her. "I already made the appointment."

Right now, she's reclining on her beach towel, her long legs pressed together, the sun caressing every inch of her almost naked body. The white spandex string bikini clings so firmly to her double-D breasts that the swells at the sides are clearly visible, as is the slope leading to the valley of her cleavage. The fact that her nipples show through the damp spandex is a testament to the fact that showing off turns her on.

This beach is known for being one of those naughty ones, you see. Sometimes girls take their tops off. Especially on the end of the beach where we are, because it's a little cove protected by a ridge, invisible from the highway. So sometimes girls take their tops off here. Sometimes girls take *everything* off here.

It's not, strictly speaking, legal. But nobody ever seems to get caught.

And nobody ever gets caught or cited for standing up on the ridge overlooking the protected cove with a digital camera and zoom lens. Before we came here, I took Bridget to those websites, paid the $20 monthly fee, showed her all the digital snapshots of women just like her at this very beach.

Now, there's four or five beach beauties, scattered around us, all semi-clothed. In bikinis, mostly, though one of them is wearing a one-piece. None of them are topless. Bridget is the best-looking one here, and her bikini is by far the skimpiest. Therefore, she's got their attention. Every last one of them. The guys on the ridge, I mean.

The eight or ten guys on the ridge *are* topless, their tacky Bermuda shorts their only clothing as their zoom lenses caress

Bridget's body. They rove over her pretty face behind her mirrored glasses. They delve deep into her cleavage, tease her nipples beneath the spandex. Ease down her tanned belly and touch the top of her thong, less than an inch above her clit, which I know is swollen and aching.

When she rolls onto her belly, they take pictures of her glorious ass, zooming in closer as she spreads her legs. The other girls watch, fascinated, some perhaps tempted to put on their own display—but most of them disgusted with the men on the ridge. None of them knows how wet Bridget is getting.

But I know.

I reach out and tug at the knots of Bridget's bikini top. She looks up at me, a little frightened, her skin reddened by the heat of the sun and the heat of her excitement. I undo the first strap, the one around her back. Then I undo the one at her neck.

The guys snap pictures, never taking their zoom lenses off of her.

I rub suntan lotion into Bridget's bare back. I sweep her long dark hair out of the way, caress her neck. I bend down low and whisper, "Sit up."

"I can't," she says. "I'll be on the web in fifteen minutes."

"That's right," I say. "Those beautiful tits for every guy to see. Jerking off on his computer screen. All over your tits. Thousands of guys coming on your tits."

That does it. Breathing hard, Bridget sits up, and now every guy on the ridge is snapping pictures of her bare tits. Her breath comes quicker, nipples hardening visibly as I kneel behind her and reach around, not wanting to spoil the view of the lechers up on the ridge. I spurt sun-warm suntan lotion onto her tits, and she starts to rub it in. I spurt more, shooting virtual cumshots for guys to watch, each one adding his own as he leers at Bridget's gorgeous breasts. We get nasty looks from the other women as Bridget rubs suntan lotion into her nipples.

"Let's go to the van," I tell her. "I think they've seen enough."

Bridget covers up with her bikini top, clutching it to her tits but not putting it on as we walk up the path.

When we make it to the van, the guys on the ridge start to clap for us. I push Bridget into the car and pull the curtains, bending her over the back seat. The bikini top falls away and I reach under Bridget to fondle her tits. She moans as I pinch her nipples, and I see camera lenses trained on our window.

I pluck her thong out of the way, tuck it to the side, enter her smoothly. She moans as I fuck her. Her hand works into her bikini bottoms and rubs her clit until she comes. I pull out of her and Bridget rolls onto her back. I mount her with my cock between her tits, and she pushes them together as I begin to fuck her, her breasts slick from suntan oil and my cock slick from her pussy. She cradles my cock and I pump her until I'm ready to come. She looks up at me as she jerks me off, and my hot streams of come join the remnants of the suntan lotion. She smears my come over her breasts, moaning softly. The men are still taking snapshots outside, but they can't see Bridget, sprawled on the floor of the van, covered in my come. That's the greatest thing about it: as much as they want this particular snapshot for their web sites, it's reserved for me.

Bridget says: "We'd better get going. It's a long drive home."

"Let's get a motel and stay another couple of days," I tell her, smiling.

Cleavage Is A Girl's Best Friend
by Rachel Kramer Bussel

I'm in my room, getting dressed. First I pick up the purple, lacy bra, the one I know is slightly too small on me. I like the way it pushes my tits together, creating cleavage out of empty space, forcing my breasts to curve outwards. I like my body okay, as much as the next girl, but for me, my breasts are my prized possessions, and I try to show them off whenever I can. I adjust the bra to my liking, then put on a low-cut black sweater which reveals just the right amount of skin, and an occasional peek at the bra beneath, if I move the right way. I squeeze into my dark blue jeans, add my black open-toed three-inch heels, and after making sure it all works in the mirror, I'm ready to go.

When I walk out the door, I know that the first thing people will notice is my cleavage, jutting forth beneath my shirt. Even though there's a slight chill in the air, I don't wear a coat. Tonight it's all about getting noticed, by anyone and everyone. I want my efforts to pay off, with appreciative glances and roving eyes as my prize.

I head over to my local bar, knowing that this being Friday, it will be a busy night. I get a cold beer and sit down at my favorite spot at the end of the bar, where I can watch all the goings on without seeming like I'm all that interested. I sip my beer and try to decide whose eye I want to catch.

I scan the room until I come to Her. She's wearing a leather jacket, dark jeans and black boots, and looks like she's never been afraid of anything or anyone in her life. I stare at her, hard, until she looks up and notices me. Even from across the room, her eyes graze my body, up and down and back, settling upon my noticeable chest. I smile, ever so slightly, then look away. I finish my beer and order another one, trying to find something to do besides fidget and stare.

Then I feel someone behind me, and hear a slight commotion. I turn around and there she is, in my corner. "Hi," she says, her voice husky and deep.

"Hi," I reply, faltering slightly, my bravado fading into nerves and the reality of my heart beating triple time.

She leans over, her chin on my shoulder, invading my space because she senses that I want to be invaded. "What's your name?" she whispers into my ear, and that mundane, age-old question suddenly become the hottest thing I've ever heard.

"What's yours?" I ask, running my hand down the length of her leather-clad arm, until I reach her hand. Because she's been so bold with me, I figure it's my turn. I lift her hand and put her first two fingers in my mouth, sucking on them. I press my tongue up against the underside of her fingers, dancing along the sensitive skin while my eyes meet hers. I've never done something like this, and I know anyone in the bar could see us, but I don't care. Tonight's my night and nobody's going to stop me from having fun.

I give her fingers a last good suck and pull them out, and she slides them along my cheek, the wetness cooling against my skin. We still don't know each other's names, but we know something much more important—that we've each found who we were looking for tonight.

She slides her still-wet fingers down my chin, past my neck, over my expanse of cleavage until she reaches my bra. She peers down to see her fingers wend their way under its lace, reaching until they hit my already hard nipple. I gasp at the feel, her rough fingers squeezing my nipple and sending ripples of pleasure throughout my body. I lean my head back a little and look at her as she delights in making me squirm. She's standing in front of me so we're slightly hidden, but I'm enjoying myself too much to really care who sees me. She takes her hand away, then brings both hands to my waist, then under my shirt. She covers my breasts, and I feel the lace from my bra rubbing against me, getting me even more excited. I wrap my legs around her, locking her in. She stays there, feeling me up, working me into a frenzy, and I wish we could just strip down to nothing right here.

The agony of waiting, of having her near and wanting to show off my body for her, is driving me crazy. I try to smile coyly, but it comes out as a moan as her thumbs press hard against my nipples. "So, could we maybe get out of here?" I ask, trying for nonchalance even though I'm sure she can feel my urgent need for her sizzling through me.

"What's your rush?" She smiles, and makes me wait for an hour, as she toys with my nipples and teases me in an unbearable yet unstoppable way. She pinches my nipples until I am contorted in agony, my pussy dripping and my total focus on the magic of her hands. She knows it too, as she surveys the room and orders a drink, continuing to pinch and pull just enough to let me know she's in charge. I don't bother asking again to leave; it will only encourage her behavior. When I start to reach under my skirt to try to provide my pussy with some relief, her hand grabs mine. She frowns at me, massaging my hand. "Not yet, my dear. You'll know when it's time. I'm just making sure you're nice and ready for me." I know that I'm ready for her this very minute, but I can't say that. So I wait, as she works my nipples into points so sensitive I can feel their heat even when she takes her hands away.

As we finally leave the bar, she puts her arm around me, pulls me toward her, and says, "You have the most amazing breasts. That's the first thing I noticed about you, although the rest of you is pretty amazing, too. I'm going to play with them all night." I smile. And with her words, I know the truth; with all due respect to the femme wisdom of Marilyn Monroe, it's cleavage that truly is a girl's best friend.

La Dolce Vita
by Sage Vivant

"No, I'm sorry. We do not have a reservation for you," the slickly handsome maitre d' announced slowly as he perused the reservations list.

Stephen had called Da Mimmo two weeks earlier to plan this evening with Brenda. The restaurant had even phoned him yesterday to confirm. As he explained this to the condescending Italian who was already eyeing the next party in line, he clenched his fists and his jaw simultaneously.

"I will see what can be done," the stuffy host promised. "Anna Lisa, would you take these people to the special lounge?" Stephen and Brenda were told to wait in the richly upholstered but dimly lit room where no other patrons kept them company.

"Why can't we just wait at the bar like everyone else?" Brenda whispered to Stephen as Anna Lisa smugly sauntered out, shutting the heavy wooden door behind her. The fireworks in Brenda's eyes blazed so brilliantly when she was inquisitive.

Stephen grinned and slipped an arm around her waist. "I'm wondering why he called this is the 'special' lounge." His mouth met hers softly, their familiar tenderness now laced with a new excitement.

To his surprise, her palms immediately found their way to his firm butt and she pushed her perky breasts into his chest. He'd expected her to protest, even if she wasn't convincing about it. Instead, her heat burned through his suit and her tongue sought his.

"We could be interrupted at any time," he warned between kisses.

"If we're good enough, maybe dinner will be complimentary," she chuckled softly.

He undressed her reverently. She never took her smoldering eyes off him. When she stood in her stockings, heels and black lace bra, he carried her to the oversized sofa and lay her down so she could watch him strip for her. Their fondness for each other mingled with sudden lust, resulting in that single-mindedness that virtually guarantees great sex.

She cupped her hands at the base of his cock and pulled him to her mouth, sucking him in slow motion, rubbing his cock over her cheeks and neck as if he were a high-priced cosmetic. He caressed her breast through her bra until her nipple pointed at him like a fingertip.

He didn't have to mention his gratitude for her lack of panties. His cock's dreamy entrance said "thank you" quite nicely. Minutes passed without either of them knowing how he started on top of her yet ended with her on all fours, pushing her shapely, ample ass at him while he cleaved it in long, loving thrusts. Her scent filled the room, overcoming the delicious aromas from the distant kitchen.

As her juices coated the insides of her thighs and slicked up his balls, the couple found themselves on the expansive, white marble coffee table, he on his knees and she with her feet on the cool stone surface, riding him with sweet relentlessness. Her eyes rolled backwards, followed by her head until the muscles of her cunt squeezed him and her shouts filled the room. Her pleasure triggered his own and the liquid heat between his legs shot skyward, filling her, mixing with her cream for a concoction all their own.

"Tandy, party of two," floated through the room from well-hidden speakers. Giggling, they dressed for dinner.

Canvas
by Renee Roberts

Rose says her body will be completely covered by the time she dies. She says this while she files her short nails. She's seated behind the counter at the bar, and I steal longing glances at her. Fantasizing.

Sometimes, when I touch myself at night, I imagine that *I'm* the one covered with ink. My body, a canvas, blank and ready for a master artist to decorate with the scenes from my dreams.

Before I go to the Radiant Room, I stroke gold-dusted blush along my cheekbones, arch my thick, dark eyebrows with pencils, fill in my full lips with a black cherry gloss. My reflection mocks me from the mirror over the sink. I don't care. I play with my thick, peasant hair, whipping my vibrant ebony wisps until they stand, glossy and high, in a 50s-style do. I turn myself into the opposite of my love, ending up looking like a Puerto Rican Elvira.

I scare all of the boys away. Don't want them. Don't care.

I want *her*.

She is my opposite in appearance. Her platinum hair is short and straight. Her eyes are a blue opaque. Her skin, what you can actually see of the flesh, is translucent white. I am dark skinned with black, shiny eyes and a trembling hand that reaches out to hand her the money for my drink. She is a dom. She doesn't even look at me.

I want her.

I dream of her inking me, of her using a silver-tipped needle to draw along the lines of my back, to turn me into a work of art. I envision the designs that would cover my skin, the cliched images: a heart with a scroll that says her name; a dragon whose wings would beat whenever I flexed my muscles; a snake with rippling, iridescent scales on its belly.

I get just drunk enough to confess these desires to Rose one night, late one night, when she's ready to go. I catch her before she pushes through the Exit, catch hold of her arm and whisper these things to her. Crazy visions. Lustful needs. She looks at me without recognition. Then she smiles, grasps my hand, and leads me after her.

We ride her Sportster to her apartment. We climb the wooden stairs in silence. We undress with only the streetlight illuminating our bodies. She laughs at my nakedness. She is always clothed, her body is always kept warm by the pictures on her skin. But her laughter isn't mean, it's gentle, ribbing. She pushes me onto her bed, heats my skin for me with her generous weight, rubs herself on me like a cat. I swivel my hips beneath hers, wondering how we're gonna do it. Wondering if she's got toys, strap-ons, dildos. She doesn't make a move to get anything. She uses her mouth on me, but not on my pussy. She uses her tongue to bathe me, to lick my naked skin, to kiss the soft places on my body: under my arms, under my breasts, the backs of my thighs.

Then, when I think I will go mad if she doesn't fuck me, she brings her mouth to my cunt and spreads warmth there, tickling me with her tongue, plunging her fingers into both my holes, telling me to make noise for her, telling me that she likes noisy girls.

I howl for her, I give her everything she asks for. I mew and cry and rock my hips back and forth on her fingers and thumb. I beg for her to fist me, and she does, expertly, ramming me in and out, driving me. I'm able to turn over, to grab onto her headboard, and I steel myself and take it, take it, while she describes the tattoos she'd like me to have: locks of silver ink around my waist, a sign on my back proclaiming me to be hers. She paints pictures with her words until I see this new reflection of myself in the mirror over the bed. I can see two tattooed bodies, hers and mine, no blank skin between us, no empty canvas.

In the morning, when the sun wakes me up, she's gone. I roll onto my side, slowly, achingly. I stand and make my way to the bathroom where I look into the mirror and see the black markings she's penned on me, all over me, the visions, the dream-like images she's drawn while I slept.

Package Deal
by Alex Reed

You're bent over my lap, your ass high in the air. You're stark naked, your body slim and helpless in my grasp. It's time for you to get what you deserve.

I run my hand up the inside of your thigh, feeling you quiver with anticipation. I know you've longed for this moment as much as I have, but even so I can sense you're very nervous.

I touch your pussy, stroking your moist slit up and down. Your clit is very firm, erect with arousal. I slip two fingers into you and you moan in response. I finger-fuck you just enough to get you going—just enough to make you want more.

Then I push your thighs open wider.

The first blow lands on your sweet-spot, a loud, open-handed blow that makes you jump. No doubt you can feel my hard cock against you, and I wonder if it makes you want to be fucked. I spank you again and this time you don't jump; you sink into it, moaning softly. Again, faster, alternating from cheek to cheek as you squirm and writhe in my grasp, whimpering "No, no, no, no!"

That makes my cock even harder. Hearing you plead with me to stop, knowing there's no way that I will. Not until you've come.

I spank faster, hitting harder, concentrating on the areas I know will drive the vibrations right down into your cunt, into your clit. Your pretty butt wriggles back and forth, the butterfly tattoo serving as a perfect target on one cheek while the swiftly-reddening curve of your sweet spot beckons me to the other. I grasp your hair with one hand and spank from one cheek to the other, pulling your head back while you whimper, "No, Daddy, no, no, no, no, no!"

I feel your cunt—wetter than ever. I finger you some more, two fingers this time, opening you up. When I start spanking you again I make sure the flat of my hand strikes your pussy. You shriek, "No, no, no, no, no!" even as you push your ass high into the air. I move back to your sweet spot and it's that combination that drives you closer. I can tell you're going to come.

I let go of your head and reach under you. I stroke your breasts, pinching your nipples, knowing that the combination will bring you over the edge. When you come, you desperately grasp the legs of the chair and beg me all through your climax: "No, no, no, no, no, Daddy, don't make me come!"

I slide my fingers into your pussy so I can feel the quivering spasms that come with your release. You're whimpering deliciously, your body rubbing against my hard-on.

I pick you up in my arms and lay you out on the couch. Spreading your legs, you lift your ass into the air, asking for something different this time.

I open my pants and mount you from behind. Your pussy is so wet that it envelops my cock hungrily, clenching tight around it even as the post-orgasmic spasms go through your snug channel. I fuck you fast, not caring to make you come—this is for me, our agreement: I spank you and you let me fuck you. But you do come, unexpectedly, pushing desperately back onto my cock, lifting your ass high, rising up onto all fours and arching your back. I feel the spasms, hear you moaning—a telltale sound that no woman can fake. You're still fucking yourself onto my cock when I erupt inside you, my come filling you.

I pull out of you, come around to the side of the sofa, and let you lick me clean.

I tuck my cock away and run my hands over your backside. It's red, hot to the touch.

"Next week, same time?" I ask.

You flush, your face red as you smile.

"Um...I don't know if I can wait that long. I was thinking, maybe, Thursday? About 4:00?"

You give me a flirtatious wink.

I chuckle.

"Remember," I say, "It's a package deal. You want this ass of yours treated right, you've got to treat my cock right."

You nod, eagerly. "Yes," you say.

"Not just your pussy," I say. "If I'm going to make time in my schedule...."

I let the demand hang in the air as my thumb teases open your lips. Your tongue slips out and licks the tip of my thumb.

"If I'm going to make time in my schedule," I say, "I want to see what this pretty mouth of yours can do besides say 'No.' Understood?"

Blushing gorgeously, you nod. And smile.

I cup your ass in my hand, feeling how hot and firm it is.

"See you Thursday?"

"Come around the back," you say. "My husband will be playing cards on the side deck."

"Sure thing," I say, and leave you there stretched out on the sofa, ass red and pussy filled with my come.

Life Lines, Love Lines
by Jennifer Smith

Deirdre asked us to attend the party with her as back up. She had fought with one of the other attendees, and didn't want to be caught alone with her. Helena and I both said, "Sure." How often do you get the chance to go to the largest mansion in Beverly Hills. In her BMW, on the way to the bash, Deirdre said, "Just let Joelle try to start something," shaking her fist in the air for emphasis.

I didn't think Joelle would have the guts to attack, not in front of everyone. Not when her boss, her boyfriend, and many of her richest clients were surrounding her. But she did. She came right up to Deirdre and snarled at her, *truly* snarled, her teeth bared, her orange-glossed lips pulled back. While the rest of the party-goers hushed, Helena walked up and said, "Joelle, that rubber dress looks incredibly lovely on you. And those extra pounds you've added? I must say, they do wonders for your ass." Joelle didn't know what to do. She skirted away like a mouse, retreating to her corner of the room.

Helena grinned and downed another glass of champagne. I went to explore the chateau. On the second floor of the party, fortune tellers had been hired to tell guests about their futures. There was a palm reader, a woman with a crystal ball, and a tarot card enthusiast. I stood in line for the palm reader, and, when it was my turn, I sat across from her and placed my hand in hers.

"Long life line," she said, quickly, her gently calloused finger rubbing into my smooth palm, "and strong love line." I heard a tittering laugh behind me, but I didn't turn, just let the lady continue with her shtick. When it was time to leave, however, I saw Helena, champagne glass in hand, leaning in the doorway.

"What nonsense," she snorted, grabbing me around the waist for support and leaning her willowy body against mine. "Life lines...." she reached for my hand to look for herself, but I steered her down a darkened hall and into one of the many bedrooms.

"Is Deirdre okay?" I asked as Helena seated herself on the chintz comforter, kicking off her shoes and crossing her long legs beneath her silver gown. I sat in a chair nearby.

"She just decked Joelle, so she's fine now."

I made a move to stand, but Helena placed her now stockinged feet in my lap, keeping me still. She set her champagne glass on the floor and motioned for me to join her on the bed.

I moved her feet, first, and walked to the door, locking it. Then, while watching my drunken silver-clad nymph, I peeled off my tux jacket and undid my shirt. Helena giggled again, saying, "Tell me more about your fortune."

"There's love in my future," I said, undoing my slacks now, letting her see that I was packing.

"Close in your future," she agreed, hiking up her dress to reveal a silver garter belt and no panties. Keeping my pants on, I moved to her side, and she gracefully lifted her ankles and placed them on my shoulders, allowing me easy entrance to her wet and willing cunt.

"You made a spot on your dress," I admonished her, using my thumb to rub her clit while my cock stroked her insides. The altercation below had obviously turned Helena on.

"I told them I spilled champagne," she said breathlessly, rocking her hips back and forth to get the rhythm going that she likes best. She needs it steady, in long, even strokes. I know how to give it to my girl, but I do like seeing her work for it.

"What else..." she started, having a hard time forming the words, her hips doing their jiggity-bounce against that expensive comforter, her cunt closing around my cock and sucking on it as if it were a second mouth with a will of its own. "What else did the fortune reader tell you?"

"Long life line," I repeated, bucking against her, humping against her. A band had started up in the courtyard below, and I switched gears and clicked onto their rhythm, a rock 'n roll beat that was a tad faster than Helena's inner metronome. It worked to bring her to the edge of climax, but I removed my thumb from her clit, unwilling to make her crest just yet.

"Strong love line," I said softly, using the flat palms of my hands on the backs of her uplifted thighs, stroking her, gently spanking her, catching the undersides of her thighs, then her ass. The rhythm section speeded up downstairs, and I joined them, really rocking into her, now, letting her have each full stroke from the tip to the base of my cock.

She purred as she came. Her heavy-lidded eyes closed tightly, and then opened and pierced into mine. She said, "That... that was good...."

I pulled out and tucked my cock back in my drawers, liking the fact that her scent and her juices still coated it. I nodded as I said, "So, wise one, tell me the rest of my fortune, would you?"

"It's long," she grinned, fixing her dress, standing to see her reflection in the mirror. "And it's hard...." I smiled at her as she slid back into her high-heeled sandals. "And I'm in every single frame of it."

Within
by M. Christian

My five fingers, my five cocks, my five dildos, touch and probe and move, knocking to be let in—all the way in. Such a harsh word for such intimacy. Maybe "reaching"? Maybe "handling" but not fisting. Too rough, too violent.

The mechanics of it are here, on a table next to the sling or someplace near the bed: Wherever the place, they are there. Roll call: gloves (comfortable, surgical if you fancy that), lube (lots and lots and lots and lots—if you think you have enough you don't have enough), and the other things that she might need (vibrator, small whips, dildo, whatever else). These are the keys, necessary but artificial—the facts of life.

The rest, though, is not artificial—way, way beyond artificial.

My gloved hand knocks, wanting in.

Carefully, I dance with her lips, waltz with her minora, majora. She leads, naturally. She takes my hand with her cunt and shows me herself. She opens w - i - d - e, says hello, invites me in.

I bow, caress, and take a first step. One finger, with a come-hither action. Not a lot. Not a lot at all—just a first step, one finger through the threshold. I have one finger in her pussy, her cunt, her vagina. One finger inside her, feeling the heat of her, taking her temperature from inside—a special, intimate, inside.

She nods, I nod, and we take another step; both listening to the music she makes.

Two is small. Just two. Two is a little number—just one and one. I move them inside her, feeling around, getting to know this special place, feeling her interior architecture. I feel a rough spot (G), the narrowing, slick walls (to cervix), the hard jab of bone under, the tight muscles over, the way her lips move, the way they won't.

Lube and more lube. She shines, glimmers with it, looking red-mirrored with the slickness, and her own slickness as well. I note the smile she gives me, with the rise and salute of her clit. Some women like it touched, during this, some don't. I ask, and she nods, so I do: bathing her bead with a careful rotation of my thumb.

Then—three.

Still a small number, a little number. Three isn't a lot, but the tightness has started. The play of one and one and one isn't as flexible as just one, just two. It's harder to move now, but I have a feel for the land, for the flow of her lips and walls. I turn my hand, rotating it slowly, pushing gently, massaging but not forcing her muscles, cooing with a special kind of sign language to her cunt, pussy, vagina: No one here who doesn't love you, no one here who means you any harm. Let me in and we'll dance ....

Three fingers, bent together: turning slowly, pushing oh-so-gently at the strength of her cunt. Not forcing. Complying, yes; easing, yes; massaging, yes; enticing—oh, yes! She opens wider, slowly allowing me passage in. Her door yields to my three long, reaching fingers.

Inside, within, I tap her G-spot, feeling its corrugated pleasure. Within, I explore the architecture of her interior.

More lube, come conversation. I ask and she answers: all is well. I stroke and ring her clit, making her smile wide and magical.

Four. When all you have is five, four is a big number. Actually all you do have is four—five is the thumb. Four now inside. Four fingers in a squeezed duckbill, forced so my tips touch together. Four inside, pushing gently but still firmly, firm but still gentle: Inside her.

Fingers are long and thin, pointed and supple (aside from the small nuts of their joints)—I perform an origami of my own hand: collapsing it, curling my fingers, cupping her from inside, sliding and dancing within her. The hard, literal, part is next, knocking on the door, wanting to be let in.

The hard part is next. I tell her as much.

She breathes, controlling the pain and pleasure that has painted her in reflections of sweat, preparing herself for the reverse birth—taking someone in rather than pushing someone out.

The hard part is the thumb and bones of my hand, the knuckles. I watch her face, hypnotized by her beauty and bravery, amazed by the dance of delight that flickers and swells over her eyes (closed in concentration, open in amazement and near shock), lips (blowing bow kisses, hissing past the pain), and nose (buttoning with the rest of her face). Bathing her clit with my lube-shiny thumb, I ask, polite and civil, if she would be so kind as at allow me into her most inner of sanctums.

Her yes is silent but obvious: with a few gentle turns of the hand, she relaxes and allows me the space and time and delight to push those last few inches in. The hard part is over, the knuckles are through.

Welcome.

This is it: I am inside and filling. This is it, one hand within. The rest is icing on the dessert: I have to do is close my long, long (sometimes too long) fingers around my thumb. Fisting ... still too rough and violent. I am inside, within—that says it all.

I watch the pleasure and the pain (more former than later) dance on her face as I slowly, slowly, slowly turn my hand with a gentle twist, rubbing my knuckles across her G-spot.

Yes, it's my hand, my fingers, my gentle pressure behind it all—but she is in control: she can say "yes," "no," "stop," "slow," "out." I would, of course, because even though it is my hand it is her temple I am walking slowly into: a supplicant, a respective worshiper: Whatever you say, Goddess.

Then she does say it—after quakes of pounding comes paint her even more with reflective sweat she clenches down on my hand, arches her spine. She says, "Out" and I do, telling her to push against my hand, to squeeze me out as I gently withdraw.

Then I am.

I clean up, kissing her hot tummy. I rub her from breasts to legs, from arms to cheeks, from the top of her head to the dimple of her navel. I put a warm blanket over her and hold her while she drifts towards sleep, falls towards exhausted slumber.

I follow close behind, having come much deeper from my hand—from being within—than ever from my cock.

Black Magic Woman
by Anastasia Philips

Janina had always been into the occult. She'd worn witch costumes each Halloween from first grade on. She painted the walls of her bedroom black and replaced all of the normal light bulbs with red ones. Her parents, a musician and an artist, encouraged her to explore, and, when talking amongst themselves in bed at night, assured each other that she'd grow out of her witchy ways. But she didn't.

Instead, she grew into looks that continually confused her parents. Her mother took down the family photo album and paged through it, trying to find the ancestor responsible for Janina's eyes. Her eyes, a normal green at birth, gradually turned as she grew older, becoming a fiery emerald with purple rims and huge, liquid irises. Janina's mother looked for the relative who had bestowed ebony hair upon her daughter, hair that had been brown when she was born. Janina's father was a sandy, blond. Her mother dyed her grey hair the same shade of brown it had always been. But during her thirteenth year, Janina, with no assistance from dye, sprouted thick, black hair that grew quickly, until she had a coil of it she could unwrap and let hang to the ground.

By the time Janina left home for college, her friends (referred to behind their backs as "the coven"), had studied enough of the occult to be able to perform small spells. Actually, the girls studied, but only Janina could make the spells work. She was particularly good at love spells, or love potions, and all of the girls had, at one point or another, availed themselves of her services. Janina had never used a love spell herself, however. Not until she graduated from college and got her first job, one with an avant-garde 'zine called *Soiree*.

Here, she felt truly at home for the first time. The other women at the 'zine didn't comment on her clothes or appearance. In fact, many of them dressed in similarly unconventional ways. And it was here, at the 'zine, that Janina met Audrey, *Soiree*'s editor in chief.

Audrey had hair that was black on one side and pure white on the other. Audrey's eyes were like two sapphire balls. Even in dim light, they shined. When Janina and Audrey shook hands for the first time, an energy crackled between them, strong enough to send tiny bursts of light flickering from the tips of Janina's midnight hair. That made Audrey laugh and lead Janina to the safe sanctity of her mammoth, cave-like office.

"You're new," Audrey said, once both women were seated in her plush, zebra-lined chairs. Janina nodded. She could feel the heat and power radiating from her new boss, and she could also feel something else, an undercurrent of sexual desire. She'd always been able to cast love spells for her friends, now she wondered if she could cast one for herself. She stared long and hard into Audrey's eyes.

Audrey laughed again, this time so loudly that the black marble walls of her office shook and their white veins shifted in designs. "You're trying to cast a spell on me?" Audrey asked, still laughing. "You...?" While Janina searched for an answer, Audrey winked and Janina was suddenly naked. Audrey spread her arms wide apart, and Janina found herself standing, pirouetting before her boss, under no power of her own. Her pussy lips were spread apart by invisible hands, her insides were probed and prodded, then filled, as if with a thick, living cock, but no lover could be seen.

Audrey enjoyed the spectacle without moving from her chair. Through her commands, Janina was stretched out in mid-air, arms and legs apart, head back, long hair undone and floating like a dark halo around her.

Janina didn't dare speak, could not compete with a power as strong as Audrey's. Instead, she let herself enjoy the sensations... now her asscheeks were parted and a new member inserted into her asshole. These probing cocks felt almost snakelike, wiggling into her, touching all of her secret places. The invisible dildos throbbed and pulsed, changed temperature as if responding to her inner desires, glowing warm in her cunt and cool in her ass, then changing. Janina closed her eyes and basked in the feeling of being so well-filled. She opened her mouth, obeying a command in her head, and a third probing, pulsing toy filled this orifice.

Audrey clapped her hands at the spectacle, then rotated her fingers and the members inside Janina began to spin, their vibrations welling up inside her until she began to come. She opened her eyes and could see her cunt juices dropping to the floor below her. Each droplet created a rainbow of lights when it hit the floor. The effect was too powerful, and she felt herself swoon, and woke, dressed again, being rocked against Audrey's breast.

"Never try to outspell a more powerful witch," Audrey whispered.

Janina nodded and lowered her mouth onto the smooth, cool skin of Audrey's nipple, suckling, gently, until she was rewarded with a honey-sweet nectar. Audrey stroked Janina's hair softly and sighed with the pleasure of finding a like-minded black-magic woman to play with.

Obscene Phone Call
by Scott Wallace

"Hello," I say, not knowing what I'm getting into.

"Hi, who's this?" you say. I recognize your voice, which is why it takes me a minute to answer.

"The name's Carl."

"That's a sexy name. I'm Lexie. How old are you, Carl?"

"You know how old I am," I say.

You giggle, a giggle that tells me I'm not getting off that easy. Or, maybe, that I'm not getting off that hard. "No, Carl, I don't know how old you are. But I don't really care, either. What do you look like?"

"Six-one," I say as I adjust the portable headset, take the phone into the living room, and stretch out on the couch. "Long dark hair," I continue, running my fingers through my strawberry-blond crew cut. "Kind of a tall, dark Fabio look."

"Wow," you say. "What are you wearing?"

I slip my hands down past the stretched-out waistband of my sweats and adjust my cock, which is getting hard. As silly as this game is, the fact that you've just called me up to play it with no preliminaries has started to turn me on. I clear my throat.

"I'm not wearing much of anything," I say. "Um, Lexie."

"Mmmmm," you sigh. "I'm not wearing much either. Just this little tank top. You can totally see my tits through it. My nipples are all hard. I'm not wearing any underwear, either. I'm real wet. That's why I called you."

"What do you look like?"

"Five-one, long blonde hair, blue eyes, thirty-six double-D."

My head spins as I remember the last time I felt your body against mine, felt your five-eight, thirty-four-B body, ran my fingers through your close-cropped dark hair and looked into your green eyes. I smile.

"You shave your pussy, Lexie?"

"Yeah, I shave my pussy," you say. "I like it all clean. Want to know a secret?"

"Sure," I say.

"When I've just shaved my pussy I can feel my cunt rubbing against my underwear.

"You don't say."

"That is," you add almost as an afterthought, "when I wear any. Which isn't often. I like to go out without panties. You know, wear tight jeans or a short skirt with nothing underneath when I go dancing. All shaved and open. And wet. I'm always wet when I go without underwear."

"I like that," I say. "You go dancing a lot?"

"Yeah," you say. "My boyfriend doesn't know, but I go dancing and sometimes I get all nasty."

"Nasty how?" I ask.

"Nasty with my girlfriends. We make out on the dance floor. That's why I don't wear any underwear when I go dancing. Makes it easier if my girlfriends and I get all worked up and have to, you know, go into the bathroom stall."

"No kidding."

"Does that make you hard, Carl?" you ask in a breathy whisper.

"Yeah," I say, putting my hand down my pants and finding that it has, which I already pretty much knew.

"Mmmm. Just telling you about it is making my pussy wet," you tell me. "Do you have a nice big cock, Carl?"

"Yeah," I say, stroking it slowly, feeling the head rub against my sweat pants.

"Is it nice and long? How long is it, Carl?"

"Ten and a half inches," I say, wondering how many inches I've just added. I make a mental note to bring a ruler on our next date.

"Fuck," you say. "I love big cocks. Ten and a half is so fucking big, Carl. I would love to suck your cock. Is it nice and fat?"

"Yeah," I say, stroking it. "Ten and a half inches and real fat."

"Fuck," you say. "I would so love to suck that. I wish you were here so I could slide my lips all up and down it. Slide it into my mouth and down my throat. Mmmmmm. Would you like that,

Carl? Put your ten-and-a-half-inch cock all down my throat, Carl?"

"Yeah," I say. "I'd love that."

"Get all nasty with me," you moan. "Tell me how you'd make me suck your cock."

I have to grope for the words, which I guess is appropriate. "I'd, ah, I'd grab your hair and force your face down on it."

You let out an explosive sigh. "Fuck yeah," you groan. "Make me suck it, Carl, fuck my throat, oh, fuck. What else would you do?"

"Um," I say. "Slap your face with it."

"Oh fuck yeah," you say. "Slap my face with your cock?"

"Um." I'm about to say, "I guess." I stop myself just in time. "Fuck yeah. Slap your face with my cock," I say.

"Oh god, yeah," you say. "So fucking hot. Make me suck it, Carl, you're making me so fucking wet. I love sucking your cock. I always swallow, Carl, you want to make me swallow, or you want to fuck my pussy? I'm rubbing my pussy, Carl, are you rubbing your cock?"

I am. "Yeah, I'm rubbing my cock."

"Fuck. That's so hot. Are you close to shooting your load for me, Carl?"

"Yeah," I say, pumping my cock. "I'm close to cumming." I can't help but think in my mind that this kind of cumming is spelled with a "u," something I always thought was stupid until now.

"I always fucking swallow cum, Carl, when I suck cock. Do you want to make me swallow your cum or do you want to fuck this wet pussy? My wet, shaved fucking pussy is so fucking shaved and wet for you, it's wet. Do you want to fuck it?"

"Um," I say. "Fuck no. I want to fuck you in the ass."

I hear your groan and know I've hit upon a nerve. "Oh fuck, Carl, fuck no, Carl, I'm so tight back there, Carl, your big fat fucking ten-and-a-half-inch cock is too big for me, Carl, you can't possibly..."

"Shut up," I growl. "Bend over. Spread your fucking cheeks."

"But what if it's too big?" you moan.

"You better lick it and get it all slick," I growl.

"Oh God, Carl, it's too big, oh, baby, I'm parting my cheeks,

I'm spreading them open, oh, I'm so tight back there, baby, are you going to put it in? Shove it in my ass?"

"Yeah," I moan. "I'm grabbing your fucking cheeks and pulling them open and I'm fucking shoving, fucking shoving it, bitch, shoving my cock in your ass."

"Oh, fuck, Carl, it hurts so bad but I'm cumming. Oh I'm fucking cumming Carl with your cock in my ass—"

And then you do, the uncontrolled sounds of your moans matching the ones I heard just last night when I did exactly what we're talking about—minus the "bitch," plus the lube. "Fuck my ass!" you moan in the middle of your orgasm.

"Yeah," I whimper. "I'm fucking your fucking ass, fuck, fuck fucking your ass—" And then I come, hard, staining the front of my sweat pants as I listen to you finishing your orgasm on the other side of the phone. I pump my cock until it's empty and the front of my sweat pants is soaked. I let out a sigh.

"Oh, God, Carl," you moan. "You fucked my ass so good. So good, Carl...."

"Thanks," I say.

"It's a simple fact," you coo. "No need to thank me."

"When are you coming over?" I ask.

"I was too horny to make the drive," you tell me. "Thanks for taking care of that. See you in half an hour?"

"I saved you some Chinese food," I say.

"Lemon chicken?"

"Kung Pao tofu. And potstickers."

"Oh, fuck, Carl," you croon. "You know what I want. You know what I need."

"Don't forget to get gas," I say.

"Don't forget to get hard again," you tell me.

"Oh, I won't."

You hang up.

Who's There?

by Sage Vivant

Though she was center stage, Clarise received no introduction. Nor could she see her audience. As she awaited the sound of Master Don's voice, she tried to determine the number of bodies present based on the feel of the air on her body. Master Don never revealed what he had in mind for her before an evening began.

She sensed more people than she could count. No light snuck in through her blindfold, so her only gauge was instinct. Sometimes she could feel someone's breath or pick up a subtle scent. Tonight, too many sensory signals assaulted her—heat from unidentified sources, breathing from all sides, disenfranchised odors that wafted past unexpectedly. Master Don's voice interrupted her silent observations.

"This beautiful, trusting soul is called Clarise. In touching her, you express not only your appreciation of her but mine, as well. Show her what you desire about her by laying hands on it, stroking it, even squeezing it gently. Let every contact you make be a meaningful expression of respect and reverence but do not restrict yourself from any part of her."

One large, warm hand immediately found its way to her left ass cheek. It paused, as if unsure of itself, then began slow, sensual circular motions on the expanse of skin it had chosen. The touch was soothing but provocative in its tenacity.

No sooner had Clarise begun to synchronize some part of herself with the movements of the hand than another, smaller hand lifted one of her breasts as if to suckle it. Clarise caught her breath with the thought of having a breast sucked by an unknown mouth. Would Master Don allow it? She remained silent but hoped desperately for a wet tongue on her nipple.

The hand at her breast kneaded what it held, sending Clarise into dizzying waves of excitement. It caressed from the meaty underside down to eager, waiting nipple, over and over. Clarise suspected that the person (a woman?) alternated hands to achieve this effect, which resembled an eerie kind of milking. She wanted to deposit something in these affectionate hands.

Meanwhile the hand at her ass continued to circle its way around. Both her cheek and the hand grew warmer with each pass and Clarise had to restrain herself from pushing her flesh into the large, welcoming palm.

Suck my tit! Clarise wanted to call out, but knew better than to second guess Master Don's plan for her. Three new hands were suddenly upon her: one massaging the tops of her feet, another tickling her pubic hair, and the third tweaking her other nipple.

"You may use your mouth to show your appreciation of Clarise's body," Master Don announced.

Clarise nearly wept with gratitude as humidity surrounded her erect nipples, a prelude to what she knew would become hungry mouths tonguing and licking. When the first tongue encircled her aureole, the other flicked rapidly at her swollen nipple. Her knees wobbled as the mouths worked, wet and hot, distracting her from the burrowing fingers between her legs.

The Stranger

by Thomas S. Roche

Casey wandered through the gyrating crowd getting progressively more irritated. This wasn't what she had in mind when she'd agreed to go dancing with Austin for the evening. He'd recently come out—no surprise to anyone except maybe him—and was in full-on queer social butterfly mode; he'd managed to talk Casey into going to a gay bar with him. It had been fun for a while, dancing anonymously among seething hordes of gay men packed into skimpy, skintight clothes, sheened in sweat and feeling each other up.

Austin was having a great time, too, bouncing from guy to guy, flirting all over the place. But Casey had started to get annoyed when Austin's flirting had gone totally out of control—last she'd seen him, a half-hour ago, he was off in the corner making out with some dark-haired hunk she wouldn't have minded getting close to herself. In fact, she'd been flirting with him herself not long ago, half-wondering if he might be straight. The guy's interest in Austin had answered that question.

Now, Casey was tired of dancing. She was a little drunk and would have gone home except that she'd forgotten to save money for a cab ride, so she was stuck until she could locate Austin among the swarm of dancing men. She hoped he had enough cash for a taxi.

Casey stumbled toward the bathroom, noting that while the men's room was packed with flesh, the girl's room looked like a graveyard. She went in, more to get away from the crowd and noise and the smell of liquor than because she had to go. Once she was inside, though, she realized she did have to go, and headed for the single stall. She gasped when she pulled open the door—two guys were in there, one seated on the toilet seat, the other straddling him. Casey started to back away, but then the guy on top turned his head and she saw that it was Austin. The guy underneath him was the gorgeous hunk she'd spotted him with earlier.

"Casey, darling!" Austin was drunk, and his London accent always came out when he drank. "I've been looking all over for you!"

Casey scoffed, pissed off for a moment. "Yeah, but you've been looking in the wrong place. I'm not in the habit of hanging out in a guy's tonsils."

Austin was drunk enough that he didn't get the joke. The guy underneath him got it, though; he looked at Casey and smiled, his blue eyes lighting up. God, he was gorgeous. Austin reached out to Casey and grabbed her hand, dragging her into the stall with them. "I'm sorry, love, don't be mad. I've only recently become gay, and I can't help myself." Casey let Austin put his arm around her and pull her close, kissing her on the forehead like a protective older brother. "This is Colin, by the way, his name starts with a C just like yours. And he's also straight. Or at least, so he says. Just here with a friend who wanted to enlighten him to the scene. Isn't that right, Colin?"

"That's right. What was your name again?"

"Casey," she said.

"Casey. That's a pretty name. But I actually meant your friend."

Austin guffawed and made a show of pretending to slap Colin on the face.

"You fucking slut. I just told you my name fifteen minutes ago, didn't I?" Casey rolled her eyes, unable to decide if she should laugh or scream at Austin. He was so charming when he got drunk, she just let him pull her close into the stall, which meant that she was pressed against Colin's body, too. She decided to giggle—mostly of nervousness.

"If you're straight, what are you doing making out with Austin?"

Colin looked up at Casey, smiling, his eyes more gorgeous than ever. He put his arm around her, his hand resting against her inner thigh. "Austin! Now I remember. I was waiting to see if his gorgeous girlfriend would come along."

"Nice line," said Casey as her skin tingled where Colin gently gripped her thigh.

"I don't think it's a line, honey," said Austin. "Colin's been jabbering on about you. I suspect he's only been making out with me to get your phone number. Can't say I blame him."

Austin leaned into Casey and kissed her full on the lips, surprising her. She felt his tongue laze along her upper lip. It had been years since Austin and she kissed. Feeling his mouth against hers sent a surge through her, making her stiffen from the sense of taboo—she'd had a hopeless crush on Austin forever, since long before he knew he was gay. And Colin, the gorgeous Colin with the dark hair and the blue eyes, chose that moment to slip his hand up her skirt.

"Hey!" she said, jerking away from Austin.

Colin's hand slipped out of her skirt and came up to her face. His fingers felt magical as he ran them over her neck and gently tugged her downward. He was so tall that it didn't take much for her to bend her face to his; and then he kissed her, tenderly. She felt his tongue gently nudging her lips apart. She let him kiss her, feeling her drunken body sway with the electricity of it.

"Please?" he asked when he pulled back.

She felt Austin's lips against her ear, kissing her as Colin's hand trailed back down her body. Colin kissed her again as Austin nibbled her upper neck, making her knees go weak so she fell against the two of them. Colin's magic fingers were up her skirt again, now tugging her thong out of the way... And then she felt like it was all over, because when two of his fingers slipped between the lips of her pussy, Colin could tell in an instant how incredibly wet she was. Maybe it was all the dancing with gorgeous gay men in tight clothes—but Casey knew better, because she suspected she hadn't been wet when she entered the bathroom. It was Austin's kiss, Colin's touch, and the press of the two men's bodies against her. And when Colin slid two fingers inside her, her pussy hurt, hurt worse than it ever had—not because something was wrong, but because she wanted it so much.

Now Austin was kissing her, and Casey found herself lost in the textures of his lips, his tongue, in the taste of his furtive hits off other peoples' cloves and Hurricanes. Every smuggled taste of indulgence was transformed by Austin's mouth into an aphrodisiac, so much so that she didn't realize that her shirt was being pulled up, didn't even think to wonder if it was Colin or Austin pulling it up, didn't entertain the thought of stopping whoever it was. The little baby-T lifted easily above her small, firm breasts, and the lacy bra came down just far enough to let Colin get his mouth around her nipple and suck gently, closing his teeth lightly around her. Casey gasped, wanting to push him away for a second; then she felt the current running from nipples to clit as Colin sucked on one nipple and used his left hand to play with the other.

With his right, he slowly slid his two fingers in and out of her, finding her G-spot with his fingertips and her clit with his thumb. Suddenly, she realized that Austin had smoothly gotten Colin's pants open, that he had the stranger's cock in his hand, that it was big and dark and very, very hard, sticking invitingly out of white briefs. Austin was slowly jerking him off as Colin finger-fucked Casey to the point where she thought, for an instant, she was going to come.

Austin's lips left hers for a moment, his tongue slippery with her spit.

"See?" he asked. "He's obviously straight. Tell you what, Colin... Pretend it's my cute little friend here sucking your dick."

With that, Austin wriggled his way down between them, getting on his knees between Colin's splayed legs as Casey leaned forward and felt a third finger entering her, gently nudging her open and pressing her G-spot as he worked her clit. She slumped against Colin, feeling him suckle her breasts as she whispered into his ear "Right there, right there," and then she saw her best friend's head bobbing up and down in Colin's lap. Casey wished she were him, wished she could get down on her knees and suck this gorgeous stranger's cock... but she wasn't, and she didn't need to be, because she was going to come any instant from the combined sensations of Colin working her pussy, clit and nipples.

She breathed deeply, smelling the liquor, cologne and sweat, and then she felt Austin's hand, taking hers and pulling it down to Colin's cock. At Austin's urging, she wrapped her hand around

Colin's shaft, feeling Austin's slippery lips against her fingers as she started jerking Colin off. She was close, damn close. And then she felt the easy pulse of Colin's cock, shooting come into Austin's mouth as Colin sucked harder on her nipples, as he pushed mercilessly on her G-spot and clit—and feeling Colin climax in her hand, feeling warm semen dribble out of Austin's mouth and around her fingers, sent Casey over the edge, making her come so hard she started moaning at the top of her lungs.

She fell hard against Colin, his big, muscled body supporting her as Austin finished him off, licking him clean as Casey's hand slipped away and came up to caress Colin's hard chest through the skintight black top.

"See?" murmured Austin, his voice rough. "Totally straight."

Casey was still panting. Outside, she could hear the DJ announcing last call.

Casey looked at Colin, nervous and a little surprised. He smiled, and his bright eyes danced as he shrugged.

"So what do you say?" laughed a very drunken Austin. "One last drink? Oh, I forgot, I just had one. Ba-dum-bum."

Casey bent forward and kissed Colin on the lips.

Lipstick Lover
by J. Nelson

This shade of red is perfect for my complexion. A true, blue red that always makes me feel completely in charge when I wear it. The color is less perfect for his complexion, but that doesn't mean I don't have fun slicking the glossy stick over his pouty lips. They *are* pouty. You can't tell that at first, not when he's in his normal "man" role without any cosmetic enhancement. Then, you simply think he has a nice smile, a gorgeous smile, with perfect lips, but not ones that you'd necessarily categorize as "pouty."

We discovered that together. We discovered just how feminine his features can be when I doll him up. How exciting it was that first time. Pouring over the different glosses in my collection, uncapping each tube and testing the hues on the back of his hand before finally coming up with this one—my favorite—the one we should have started with in the first place.

Now, we have a routine down. It used to be a little varied each time: would we go the whole route? Eyeliner and mascara, foundation and blush? Occasionally. Every once in awhile for really big scenes. But what we learned over time and experimentation is that what we both really like is the lipstick. The sensation of applying it and kissing it off again.

Or having him kiss the lipstick away on my skin, making a road map of pleasure as he moves from one place on my body to another. I like to watch in the mirror as he takes his time decorating my breasts with his lipstick kisses. I tremble as he leaves those kissmarks in a line down my belly, creating a glistening red smear as he heads to his final destination.

We take breaks during the evening, with me reapplying the color to his pout, knowing full well that all the dark, rich pigment will be spread along my sheets and skin by the end of the night.

He holds still, as still as he can, as I apply the color. The action is an immediate turn-on for him. I can see his erection straining

through the thin fabric of his boxers—kiss-printed boxers that I
bought him last Valentine's Day.

    Turns me on, too—

    Can't say why. It just does.

Ticklish Mary
by Albert Simmons

She's very ticklish. As my hand gently caresses the small of her back, she shivers in my lap and whimpers slightly. She wants to beg me to stop. But she knows better.

"You've been very bad, Mary, haven't you?"

"Yes," she whispers, her naked body stretched gloriously over my lap, her smooth, round cheeks presented for my punishment. I can see the perfect tattoo just at the top of her rear furrow: My signet, inscribed elegantly in blue-black. "I've been very, very bad."

"Why don't you tell me how bad you've been?"

"I didn't want to—" she breathes, wriggling in my grasp as I run my hands up the backs of her slender thighs. Her pussy lips are swollen, arousal showing in the glistening moisture forming between them. "I didn't want to, but I touched myself."

"You did, did you? Do you mean you touched yourself, or you fucked yourself, Mary?"

Mary twists in my lap and buries her face against my side.

"Tell me."

"Yes," she says. "I fucked myself."

She loves to play shy. I love to coax it out of her. "Tell me about how you fucked yourself, Mary," I tell her. "Did you fuck yourself with a really, really big cock?"

"It....it was the dildo you left me," she says. "The one you told me not to use."

"Tsk, tsk," I say. "That one's much too big for you. I told you to wait until I could show you how to use it properly." My hand comes to rest on her pussy, and I gently begin to fondle her pierced clit with the tip of my finger. She mewls deliciously, grasping my leg as sensation flows through her.

"I know," she says. "But I was so horny. I was thinking about you."

"What were you thinking about me?" I ask her.

"Thinking about your cock."

"What did you want to do to my cock?"

"Suck it," she sighs as I tease apart her swollen cunt-lips. I slide two fingers into her center and feel how wet it is. She groans, loudly, her voice cracking as she gasps out: "I wanted to suck your cock."

"Tell me all about it. Tell me how you fucked the big cock I told you not to fuck."

Mary's gasping for each breath as I finger her, the tips of my index and middle fingers rubbing just the right spot to make her come. I can tell she's having a very hard time speaking, but I love to hear her struggle to find the words.

"I was so horny," she coos. "I was thinking about sucking your cock. How much I like sucking your cock. And you'd left me that big fat dildo and I wanted it. It's almost as big as your cock. I know I had the smaller ones you said I could use, but I wanted *that* one. The big one. Because I wanted to suck your cock so bad, and I couldn't, because you weren't there."

It's been a full week since Mary and I have seen each other; I had to go away on business, and I left her with an impressively large dildo—which, for the record, is considerably thicker than my cock, though shorter. I told her not to use it, anticipating that if she did, this very scene would ensue.

"So you sucked the dildo, didn't you, Mary?"

"Uh-huh," she nods, moaning. "I just wanted to suck it a little. I told myself it was okay. You'd said not to fuck it, not to put it in my pussy or.....my back door. So I figured it was okay if I sucked it. But once I got my lips wrapped around it—"

I start to pump my fingers harder in and out of her pussy, knowing that telling me about her transgression is turning her on. I tease her clit with my other hand, until I sense that she is very close to climax. I move my hand up and begin tickling the small of her back again, making her yelp in surprise. Being tickled while she's on the edge of orgasm drives my sweet Mary absolutely insane.

"Tell me," I say. "Tell me what happened."

"Once I got my lips wrapped around it," she moans. "I couldn't stop. I wanted it so bad. I wanted your cock, but you weren't there. So I started to fuck myself with it. I hardly even knew what I was doing. I just did it," she moans, pushing herself desperately back onto my fingers. She's on the edge, and I slip my fingers out of her pussy and grab her sides, beginning to tickle her. She shrieks and fights to get away. I flip her onto the sofa and push her down with my knee on her ass, feeling the moisture of her pussy soak through the knee of my jeans. She goes rigid, her panting breaths coming short. I begin to trace gently, lightly, down her back again, barely touching the sides, making her flesh twitch. I hear a long, low wail, plaintive and suffering, erupt from her mouth, and she begs me: "Please...."

"Do you think you should be tickled?" I ask her. "Or fucked?"

"Fucked," she whimpers desperately. "Please, fucked. I need to be fucked. I've been wanting your cock for so long....please....!"

Holding her down, I grab her sides and tickle her mercilessly. She shrieks, great shuddering gasps that could never pass for laughter mingling with the faintest of giggles as she struggles against my weight and determination.

"You've already been fucked," I tell her, stopping for a moment.

"Yes," she whimpers, her voice muffled by the sofa cushions. "I couldn't help myself. I fucked myself with it. I wanted your cock so bad."

I reach for the sides of her waist again, and she gasps, afraid I'm going to tickle her again. But I grasp her hard, lifting her hips up and shoving a cushion under her waist so her ass is raised high in the air. I open my pants and take out my cock, and without teasing her I slide my cock into her pussy.

"Oh, God," she sobs into her sofa cushion.

I slide into her with rhythmic thrusts, bringing her close, feeling her pussy tense as she approaches orgasm. I sense her reaching for it, striving, trying too hard to grasp onto it so she can come. But she's groping too desperately, her muscles tight from the tickling, her pussy clamped too firmly around my cock for her to come. She strives after it, humping herself back onto my cock, wanting it more than she's ever wanted an orgasm in her life. I decide to break her concentration. In a rush, I grab her sides, tickling violently, making her scream at the top of her lungs just as she loses control of her orgasm—and then, unexpectedly, her orgasm overtakes her like a crash of waves, and I feel her spasming underneath me, losing control totally as I pound down into her.

And she does lose control, as I feel hot streams shooting out onto my legs. The feel of her spurting doesn't make me slow; on the contrary, I keep tickling and pounding her, fucking so hard she slams into the arm of the sofa, so hard I think I hear it cracking.

Then I come, still tickling her, feeling her thrash back and forth under me. The sofa cushions are wet—but I don't care. She lies inert underneath me, moaning. Almost sobbing. Every time I shift atop her, she gasps as if I'm going to tickle her again. It excites me to be so in control of her, so totally dominant over her universe.

"Oh, God," she moans softly.

"You begged to be tickled," I remind her.

"Yeah," she sighs, wriggling under me. "I begged to go to grad school, too, but that doesn't mean I looked forward to writing my dissertation."

"Good point," I say. "But did you come good?"

"Oh, God," she moans. "Oh my fucking God."

"Sounds like a yes," I tell her, envisioning many more ticklish encounters with Mary in the future.

Everything Old
by Serina Jurgens

I work at an antique store on Fourth Street. We carry mostly knickknacks and old clothing, period pieces. We're pretty busy right before Halloween, when the richer women stroll in, looking for something classy (and sexy) to wear to their husbands' office parties.

I was reading a book one evening, right before closing. The bell at the door tinkled and I looked up to catch a beautiful blonde walking in. She had on a black suit and her shining hair was back from her face in a French twist. She seemed to know the layout of our store as if she were a regular costumer. Without a word to me, she headed straight to our rack of old petticoats and slips, pulling the two most expensive ones from the back.

I checked the time. It was five minutes to closing. A customer with such divine tastes deserved personal service. Quickly, I walked over and locked the door and lowered the shades.

"You can try those on here," I told her, motioning to one of our big wardrobes with a full-length mirror.

She hesitated for a moment before removing her clothing. She had that pale skin that works so well with white underclothes. I could see the fine tracery of blue veins beneath the surface of the skin on her neck, chest, breasts.

"What do you think?" she asked when she had the old-fashioned garments in place.

I shook my head, speechless. She'd made the total transformation from business woman, sleek and refined, to Victorian character... I don't know what precisely. Chambermaid? Whore? My mind worked swiftly to try to classify her, but I failed.

The laces in the back of the corset were still undone. I walked over to her and began to fix them for her. As I tugged at the ribbons, she sucked in her breath, making her stomach concave.

"Tighter?" she asked, a rushed whisper of breath. I pulled the ribbons harder, then fastened her up, my hand lingering on the sweet curve of her back when I was done. She met my eyes in the mirror. She looked over to the rack of canes in the umbrella stand by the door, then back at me. I know all about looks like that. Without a word, I crossed the room, grabbed one, and told her to assume the position. I wasn't sure precisely where the words had come from, they were suddenly in my head.

"It's been a long time..." she said as she bent her slender body and grabbed her ankles. I lifted the petticoat and tucked it into the waist of the garment, revealing her supple thighs, her naked ass.

"Too long," I agreed, going with that inner script. "I'll give you twenty strokes. Move before I'm finished and you'll get ten extra."

"Yes, Mistress," she said, and that word sent something dark and silver through me. I began her whipping, catching her at the fullest part of her ass, the curves of her upper thighs, marking her well. Lining one blow below the next. She took the strokes silently, didn't flinch, didn't beg. I felt myself growing wetter as her ass became a dark blushing cherry.

Tears lined her face by the time I was finished, but she didn't move. I carefully led her to one of our lounges and laid her out on her stomach, going to work from behind, parting the rosy-hued cheeks of her ass and plunging into it with my tongue. Delving into her dripping cunt with my fingers and then painting her skin with her own sticky juices. She drew in her breath when I touched each line from the cane. I pinched the welts between my fingers, using my free hand to tickle her clit at the same time. I gave her the dark mix of pain and pleasure that I could tell she needed. A power built inside me as I worked her; the shudders that ran through her body told me I was playing my role to perfection.

She came as silently as she'd taken her whipping. She trembled all over, and I thought I could see a bright white halo of electricity around her, but when I blinked, it was gone. When she rolled over, I saw that her face was clear, no tear stains, no flushed cheeks. She stood and adjusted herself, then returned to the rack of clothing, lifting a red dress and sliding it over her head. The dress fit her as if it had been cut specifically for her body.

"It's been a long time since I had this on."

"A fancy dress?" I asked, coming over to her, standing behind her with my hands around her waist, then sliding one up to rest it on her cheek.

"*This* dress..."

She tilted her head and stared at my reflection in the wardrobe. My hand was still on her skin, her noticeably *cold* skin. A tremor ran through me. "We got that piece in yesterday," I told her. "From an auction house. It was supposed to have belonged to..."

"Sapphire Sam," she said, "I know." She undid her hair and let her mane loose over her shoulders. Everything about her gleamed—her skin, her eyes, her teeth when she smiled at me.

Exploring Psyches
by Sage Vivant

"Denebria, while I don't doubt that your powers of seduction are formidable, I think it's unlikely that a grown man can ejaculate just from your touch through his clothes," Rick pointed out.

"Why would I make it up? Wouldn't it be silly for me to lie to my shrink?"

He stared at her as he often did when he wanted her to continue. She decided to volley back some silence of her own, wondering who would break first.

"Show me how you pleased that man," he said finally. His voice was darker, deeper than normal.

At first, she remained in her seat, uncertain and disbelieving. To imagine that this man, the object of her forbidden fantasies, now seemed to be asking her to touch him, immobilized her. He stared more intensely at her until his gaze willed her to walk to him.

"Well, I was kissing him first," she explained in a tremulous whisper.

He tilted his face upward as he put his clipboard on the nearby table. She bent to kiss him and as their mouths yielded to one another, his palm caressed her breast. Her own hand moved quickly to his bulging crotch.

As she palpated his balls, he squirmed slightly and moaned into her mouth. He spread his knees further apart, and with his free hand, he buried his fingers in her hair.

What were previously loose pants were now tight. He was enormous under her skillful strokes and the more she touched him, the more obsessed she became with seeing what she had so successfully aroused.

He pulled away from her lips gently so he could speak to her. "Strip for me, Denebria. I need to see you." She had never heard such urgency from him before.

"But what about our, uh, test?" She looked down at his swollen lap, continuing to work what she hoped was magic.

"Please. Just take your clothes off."

She removed her hand and stepped away to stand before him. He replaced her hand with his own, a sight she found erotic in the extreme. As he sat there, expectant and wide-eyed, thighs parted like a wishbone, she pulled her jersey over her head.

"Oh, Denebria. Those big, beautiful tits. You have no idea how often I think about them," he told her, breathless as he rubbed himself.

She unhooked her bra to unleash its contents. As her breasts bounced free, he bit his lip. He cried out softly as she stepped out of her pants to reveal her belly ring and she realized he was filling his crotch with the hot come she'd inspired. She now stood before him in only sandals and panties. Soaking wet panties.

"But that doesn't count," she teased. "You did that yourself."

"No," he grinned, still panting. "You can take full credit for that one."

She took his hand to pull him to his feet. Once he stood, she stripped him, revealing the smooth, hard chest and the thick, come-covered cock. She knelt to clean him with her tongue before he joined her on the floor. When he ate her, she creamed his face with months of pent-up pleasure, and when he slid deep into her pussy, she thought of nothing except the fire beneath his skin.

Ashley's Secret
by Diane Chalk

Ashley had dated Peter for two months before coming to terms with the fact that there was no chemistry between them. There'd been no spark with her and Robert, either. Or the man she'd met on vacation in Paris. Or the boys who had thronged around her in high school, dying to take her out on a date, to the movies, or to the prom.

But Peter had seemed different from the rest. At least, at first. He didn't pressure her, didn't call too often, didn't act demanding about sex or kissing or anything. When they were out, Ashley enjoyed herself, but in the way she enjoyed hanging out with friends. Nothing more... until, she met Peter's sister.

Then, suddenly, Ashely's emotions, usually so controlled, so easily kept under wrap, began to play nasty tricks on her. At dinner, with Peter's sister across the way, winking at her, bumping her feet beneath the table, Ashely felt herself blush. Her heart raced. Her mouth was unable to formulate words of pleasant conversation when Peter's mother spoke to her.

Ashley's discomfort was not lost on Gemma. Peter's sister had a sense about things, about people, and she knew Ashley was interested in her from their first glance. Now, Gemma was simply making the connection clear, paving the way to Ashley's introduction in the ways of Sapphic love. After dinner, when the family moved to the living room for glasses of brandy, Gemma seated herself next to Ashley, and, on the pretext of showing Ashley their family photo album, Gemma moved closer until they were hip-to-hip.

Ashely saw none of the photos, none of the sweet family ski pictures, happy images captured forever by Kodak. Ashley let Gemma turn the pages, telling stories about the different locations, their vacation to Mammoth, the time in Hawaii when the rain never stopped, and Ashley nodded, wondering if the room was overly hot, or if her inner temperature had gone haywire. Gemma understood the way Ashley was feeling, and she kept up her steady monologue of relatives and faraway places, until, sensing that Ashley was on the verge of passing out or *freaking* out, she suggested they go up to her old bedroom, where the rest of the albums were kept.

"You don't mind, do you, Peter?" Ashley asked, her voice wavering. He was watching the game with his father, and he didn't mind at all. Gemma and Ashley walked the stairs in silence, and, in silence, undressed the second the door closed behind them. Ashley wasn't sure what had come over her, but she knew she needed to be in Gemma's arms, and she wasn't going to let herself, her calm rational self, keep this need from being fulfilled.

She tried to speak, to ask Gemma questions, but the other girl shook her head, placed her finger on Ashley's lips, then covered those pretty pink lips with her own mouth, silencing her.

Ashley closed her eyes and let Gemma take over, let Gemma lead her to the bed, covered with a blue flannel blanket. Let herself be spread out on the bed, her legs splayed, her hair falling around her shoulders, but not hiding her breasts. Her nipples were hard. Gemma licked them, kissed them, suckled from them. Ashley cradled Gemma's head in her hands, losing herself in the sensation of being treated warmly, softly, as she'd always fantasized about.

Gemma covered Ashley's body with her own, letting Ashley become used to the feline feeling of another's woman's body. It was right to be doing what they were doing. It was perfect, Ashley assured herself. Nothing, not holding hands with a man, not being kissed by a man, not being fucked by a man, nothing had ever come close to giving her the amount of pleasure that Gemma was with the pressure of her body alone.

Ashley was courageous and began to stroke Gemma's back, curving her hands into cups over Gemma's hips, then moving lower to stroke the woman's ass. It was divine, exploring the dips and curves of her new lover's body. She wanted to explore her forever, lose herself in Gemma's warmth.

They were in a sixty-nine, dripping juices into each other's mouths, when they heard footsteps in the hall. There was a knock, and Gemma called out, "Hold on! One sec!" and the women scrambled into the clothes, looking disheveled, but dressed, when Peter opened the door and walked in. He leaned against the wall, a smile on his handsome face.

"I knew it," he said to Ashley, "I knew you'd like Gemma..."

Ashley stared at him, her eyes wide.

"I've got a secret of my own that you two can help me with... I need to introduce mom and dad to my lover... Kirk."

Birthday Spanking
by Mark Williams

Harriet was known as one of the biggest bitches in our company, yet I found her charming, sexy, perhaps even lonely or confused. Certainly, she had an erratic personality. She could be sweet as all hell to me one week, then not even look at me or talk to me the next. Still, when she got really dressed up for work, which was about half the time, she looked damned hot.

The thing was, I could never tell how she was going to act toward me. Maybe that added to my interest in her. And I knew her birthday was approaching, meaning her behavior might be even more unpredictable. On the day of, I took a chance and left a red rose on her desk—anonymously. This threw her into a tizzy, as she couldn't imagine who could have done such a thing.

Finally, she glided over to my desk, looking spectacular. "Mikey, did you see anyone over by my desk earlier?"

"No," I answered honestly. "But the rose is from me."

She was startled and actually blushed. "Well, that was sweet of you. I never expected..."

"And I'd be happy to throw in a little birthday spanking with it, if you like," I whispered in my lowest possible voice.

"Excuse me?" she said, making me suddenly nervous. "Did I hear you correctly?"

"I hope so."

"The only thing you're going to spank is your monkey, pal," she said in her bitchiest tone, before adding almost coyly, "and I'm going to watch."

My cock hardened at once. I'm sure she knew it even though my lap was concealed by my desk. "Anything you say, Harriet...just let me know when and where."

"How about right here, right now?"

My stomach tightened and my cock grew harder. "This is a little too public don't you think?" My desk was in an open area, making her suggestion far too risky to consider.

She thought a second. "I suppose so. Follow me to the 'person's room.'"

I did as ordered. Our unisex bathroom had a locking door. Perfect.

She went in first, and after looking around, I followed her in. Without a word, she leaned forward on the bathroom sink, offering her skirt-covered ass to me.

"Do you still want to spank me?" she asked. I was too embarrassed to reply or move. I never thought my joking remark would go this far, this fast. I was frozen, until she said, "Go ahead, baby. It's okay." I moved behind her and raised her skirt as much as I could. Her slip moved easily with it. Her pantyhose-covered ass beckoned me. I raised my hand and gave her a playful but gentle slap.

"A little harder, Mike," she moaned. I obeyed. She squirmed from the slap, but I couldn't help but suspect we were both enjoying ourselves. I hit her seven more times, each time a bit harder, then said, "Ummm...I don't honestly know how old you are."

"That's none of your fucking business. Give me one more hard one, and we'll call it even." I did just that, and she exhaled a loud groan. "Now it's your turn. I want you to spank yourself for me. Drop trou and do it, now!"

Given our location, there was urgency to the situation. I unbelted and unzipped my pants and let them fall to my ankles. I also pulled down my underwear. My throbbing cock sprang to full attention once released.

"Oh, yeah," Harriet smiled. "I never knew you were so big. Good for you, Mike. Now work your hand, like a good boy. This is gonna be my present."

I began to jerk off, needing no further incentive. Harriet sat back on the sink and pulled up her skirt, exposing her silky legs to me to help me further. I stood facing her, feeling foolish in my nakedness, but determined to come for her.

"Come on, Mike—"

I picked up my pace, feeling a tightening in my testicles.

"Are you close, baby?" She could see it in my face.

"Yes," I grimaced.

"Then start singing 'Happy Birthday' to me," she cooed.

I gave her a look of disbelief, yet again, somehow did as told. "Happy Birthday to you..." My balls tightened a bit more.

"Keep going, baby..."

"Happy Birthday to you...Happy Birthday, dear Harriet..." My body was in spasm. "Happy Birthday to you!" I croaked. I was in full orgasm right now, warm, white come was everywhere. Harriet slid off the sink and moved her mouth to my cock, licking and sucking up as much ejaculate as she could.

"Now I've blown out my candle," she laughed.

I was weak everywhere. "God, Harriet, you're so sexy..."

"I know. And for being such a good boy, maybe I'll plan a bigger surprise for your birthday."

I squirted a few last drops in her mouth. It had been a birthday surprise—for me as well as her.

Weather Watch
by Stefani Wheeler

The stodgy male weather reporter, whose name was something ridiculous like Autumn Wind, was replaced in mid-season by a youthful, freckle-faced redhead named Azure Kelley. I caught her for the first time on a rainy night, and I was so taken by her appearance that after the weather report was over—a full five-day forecast—I realized I didn't have a clue if the rain storms would continue or if it would finally start to snow.

It wasn't the first time I'd seen her. It was simply the first time I saw her on TV. Azure and I had been lovers once, long ago, and had split when her career became more important than her connection to me. But I hadn't forgotten her. Hadn't stopped thinking about her after all those years. Now, she was back to haunt me...on my television set.

I always like to know what the weather is going to be. My job, delivering flowers, takes me outside so often, it's important to be dressed correctly. This is what I told myself when I stayed up to catch the late-late forecast. Again, Azure pointed knowingly to the various parts of the country map. Again, I found myself lost in daydreams in which she pranced naked through her forecast, snowflakes drifting down and melting on her pale, gold-freckled body.

I had to wait until the newspaper came in the morning to get dressed. Showers were called for, and I wore my bright yellow boots and heavy-weather gear, still thinking of Azure as I drove to the shop.

She was on again that night, and I caught the newscast early enough to hear her announced as the new weather forecaster. I paid attention to what she said this time, but I did it while imagining her in the nude, spread out on a million rose petals, the red floral carpet the perfect canvas on which to display her nubile body.

In the morning, dressed in slacks and a cardigan (she'd

predicted winds, but no rain), I added a special delivery to my route. I dropped a dozen red roses at the station, signing the card with my name and number and a one-line sentence that said I missed her.

That night, watching her forecast, I was gratified to see one red bud in her lapel. And later that night, while I was curled up in bed reading a mystery, I was even happier to hear the phone ring.

She said, "Thank you for the flowers. They were lovely."

"I'm glad you liked them," I replied, my mind racing for something clever or cool to say. "Would you like to come over?" I asked, knowing it was neither clever nor cool, but what I wanted more than anything else. "I live very close to the station."

She hesitated only a second, then asked for my address. I prepared for her arrival as quickly as I could. Within minutes, there was a knock on my door and there was Azure, clad in a white, faux-fur jacket standing on my step. I hurried her inside, and then, after a brief up-and-down glance on both our parts, herded her up the stairs to my loft. She was easy to undress, a simple tug on her zipper revealed a black, lycra body suit, and that was off just as quickly. I removed my nightgown and climbed onto my bed with her, rediscovering her body with a pleasure that had no boundaries.

In the dim sheen of my one light, her freckles appeared gold-flecked, fairydust sprinkled all over her lithe form. I pressed my face to the flat of her belly and inhaled to find her deeper scent, the base scent of her gold-dripped skin. Her skin was warm beneath the palms of my hands, warmer still as I stroked her, running my palms along the full length of her body, massaging her muscles, rubbing the pads of my fingers against her ribs, between her thighs, under her hips.

I described my fantasies to her as I continued in my explorations. I sniffed behind her earlobes, smelled her amber hair, whispered to her of sweet love among snowflakes, rough love under bright, sunlit beaches. As I spoke, I sensed that she was growing wetter, and further explorations proved my forecast correct. Each story I spun for her made her a little more excited, until the dew began to form on her ginger-hued pussy lips. I left those for last, describing how I longed to spread her on a carpet of petals and have windswept, passionate sex with her until the petals crushed beneath us and released their fragrant blood around us.

At that, she hoisted her hips upward, begging with her actions and then her words for me to relieve her. Not one to keep a damsel in distress, I moved between her legs and played my role impeccably. I teased the nub of her clit between my lips. I spanked her thighs lightly while I worked her pussy hard. I followed the rhythm she set with her hips bucking on my sheets, followed with my lips clasped around her pearl. I made her come while she grabbed onto my shoulders with both hands, and in my mind, her freckles fell from her skin to my own, dusting me with their magic, golden powers, alighting on my skin like fireflies and bestowing their secret glow to me.

When I watched the newscast the next night, I knew the forecast for our future would be sunny, despite the most possible chances of snow.

Men at Work
by Alison Tyler

Maybe there's no such thing as love at first sight, but lust at first sight....well, that's a different story altogether. Because that's what I had, and I had it bad. Lust for the dark-haired, dark-eyed captain of a rough-and-rowdy road crew.

The crew had been out in our little rural community for weeks. Trimming trees. Moving boulders. And making me want to come. Not all of them. Just one of them. A fiercely handsome man with a sleek mustache and sparkling brown eyes. He'd look at me when he was the one holding up the "stop sign," and I'd look back through the windshield, flush, and look away. How many times? Three, four, every fucking time I went to do an errand. And I went to do more errands than usual when I knew they were at work. I put on elaborate make-up just to go to the grocery store. Normally a jeans-and-T-shirt-type of girl, I wore skirts and high-heeled leather boots and I took extra time styling my long black hair.

After several weeks of visual foreplay, I got bold. I held his eye contact and stared back at him, gazed through my cherry-flush, forcing the connection. He liked that. He tilted his head at me and narrowed his eyes, and I could almost hear what he was thinking. "Take me on? Is that what you think you're doing, little girl? You think you can take me?"

The men were connected to one another with walkie talkies, letting each other know when cars were waiting at either side of the road work. One afternoon, I watched a heavy-set man radio another while the stop sign was in place. After a moment, he flipped the sign to "slow," and motioned me forward. As I drove around the windy roads, I spotted a golden-yellow work truck in my rear view mirror. Was it him? How was I supposed to find out?

I kept on normal my route, saw the truck holding steady, and finally I pulled into the dirt lot of a local park. Empty. Totally empty. Surrounded by trees. Hidden. The truck pulled in behind me, and my man got out. I knew in my head what I wanted to do, but I didn't know whether people really behaved like that outside of porno movies. Could I step from my convertible, rush over, and tell him what to do to me? Turned out I didn't have to. He knew. True doms can always sniff out a sub.

With a nod of his head, he motioned for me to come toward him. I slid from my seat, slammed the door behind me, and walked to the back of his truck. As soon as I was in his range, he gripped onto my shoulders and brought me into his arms for a kiss—the kiss I'd imagined since I'd first seen him. Hot and fast, his mouth firm against mine, his teeth finding my bottom lip and then biting it hard. Then, because it had to happen, because it was right, he pushed me down on the gravel-strewn dirt and unbuttoned his deeply faded jeans. I was ready, my lips parted, mouth open, but he stopped me before I could act. Quickly, he pulled his heavy leather belt free from his jeans, and with me in the exact position he wanted, he captured my wrists tightly behind my back.

"Such a tease," he said, running his fingers roughly under my chin, tilting my head upward with a jerk. "Such a fucking tease."

I sighed, so hungry now, so desperate, but he wasn't ready to give in. All I wanted was the taste of his cock in my mouth, and I wanted it more than anything I've ever craved, yet he wouldn't let me suckle from him. With one hand still under my chin, he ran the back of his free hand against my cheek, softly, making me tremble all over at the gentleness of his touch. Then his hand came up high in the air, and he slapped my cheek, catching me off-guard, making me bite down on a moan. I lowered my head, shuddering all over, feeling how wet my panties were growing. Feeling how much I needed this. Needed him to treat me exactly how he was.

"Look at me, baby," he insisted, and I raised my head.

Now, he pushed forward, butting against my lips with the head of his cock. Oh, god, oh Christ, was I ready. I wanted to drink, wanted to drain, wanted to swallow him whole. But still he wouldn't let me. He plunged in, taking his pleasure, then slid back out and bent to rub my nipples forcefully through my thin white blouse. He pinched them hard, and I arched and groaned, and while my mouth was open, he slid his cock in again. Each time he played me, he made me wetter still. So that I didn't know what I was doing anymore. All I knew was I had the need—the urgency—to drink him down.

"Bad girl," he said, "lost in your little games. Cruising the curves in your silver convertible. And all you want is for someone to fuck that sweet mouth of yours. Isn't that right?"

I think I nodded. I know I moaned. And he let me, finally, let me have at him. I swallowed with a vengeance. I sucked and pulled, my cheeks indenting with the intensity of my hunger. He held me steady with his rough hands on my shoulders, pinned me in place in his strong grip. My eyes wide open, I saw the trees behind him, saw his scuffed workboots below, the dirt under my knees. It was a relief to be allowed to use my mouth, to trick my tongue up and down his straining rod. I almost cried with the release of tasting the first drops of his pre-come.

When I could think of nothing more than draining his every drop, he pulled out again, lifted me up by my arms, and bent me over. Holding me steady, my skirt captured up at my waist, he slid my panties all the way down my legs and waited for me to step out of them. Then he punished my naked ass with his large open hand, spanking me hard and fast. All my faith was in him. He had the total control to keep me balanced, so that I wouldn't fall forward against the gravel, so that I wouldn't collapse on the ground. I had no thoughts now; I simply let him take me. Let him push me back down again onto the scraped raw skin of my knees, so that I could open my mouth wide and suck him. Sweetly suck him. My mouth earning the pleasure of the power he imparted.

Up and down my tongue tricked against his shaft. In and out his cock plunged, searching out the warm wet heat of my throat. I was delirious with the pleasure of serving him. Breathing deeply, I memorized his smell, the way his skin felt against my cheeks, the way my ass smarted under the gauzy fabric of my summer-weight skirt. Then he was once again in motion, lifting me up and bringing me to the back of the truck. My wrists were still bound behind my back, so he had to slide my skirt up for me, kicking my legs wider apart, pushing into me with the spit-slicked length of his erection. He fucked me so hard that his truck shook. My face pressed into the metal of the truck bed; my honeyed juices spilled down my thighs. And when we were finished, he simply unbuckled the well-worn belt and set me free.

But I didn't want to be free.

"You're calmer now, aren't you, girl?"

I thought about the words before I answered, and then I nodded. He was right. All the nervous energy that had pulsed through me each time we'd made eye contact was now gone. I felt warm and in control. Better yet, I felt satisfied. I watched him get into the truck and drive out of the lot. And although I don't know when the road crew will be back, I do know that I'll be ready.

Final Exam
by N.T. Morley

Nottage & Softbottom's
Vocational Academy
of Domestic Service

Maid's Etiquette 101
Instructor: Miss Wallop
Final Examination

The following examination will count for 60% of your grade. However, as you know, only those receiving perfect scores in the class will be graduated to Etiquette 102. Those not receiving a perfect score will receive swift and extensive instruction from those who do. Rulers will be issued as soon as the grades are posted.

Please ensure that you sit up straight while writing. You will be graded on penmanship. Miss Wallop will be surveying the class with ruler in hand, so no wandering eyes, please.

Question 1.
When arriving at your new employer's home, you should ensure that:

    a) The uniform the Spanish majordomo has issued you is at least three sizes too small and missing several of its buttons

    b) The laundress at the nunnery has unfortunately forgotten to pack your underwear

    c) The condition of the servants quarters requires you to share a single bed with two identical twins named Fabienne and Kamchatka

    d) All who inhabit the household are quickly convinced that you are a virgin and begin to wickedly plot your merciless defloration and induction into the vagaries of uncontrolled amorous surrender

Question 2.
The proper posture for serving cocktails at a party where the guests are seated is:

a) Standing up straight, bent over at the waist so your skirt rides up in front of the guests

b) Offering a deep curtsey to each guest as you deliver his or her drink

c) Discovering yourself without warning being bent over the side of the sofa, savaged from behind while the guests drink straight from the bottle

d) All of the above

Question 3.
The proper posture for serving cocktails at a party where the guests are standing is:

a) Holding the tray at shoulder height

b) Holding the tray at chest height

c) Extending your pretty derriere as you walk through the crowd, so that the lustful guests may endeavor to cop a feel

d) Kneeling on the floor offering oral service with your knees in a pool of spilled liquor

e) both c) and d), depending on whether it's before or after midnight

Question 4.
The first thing you should do when a male guest enters your employer's house after a long journey is:

a) Take his coat and offer him a cocktail

b) Take his coat, offer him a cocktail and a cigar

c) Carelessly knock his umbrella out of his hand, offering a thin excuse for you to bend over and retrieve it, accidentally rubbing your sassy behind against his rapidly swelling man-thing, you shameless trollop

d) Let the butler get the drinks and smokes; offer the poor chap a blowjob, for the love of God!

Question 5.
As a group, male chauffeurs tend to prefer:

a) Fervent oral service offered by a tawdry minx such as yourself

b) The forbidden excesses of rear-passage bliss

c) The rutting heat of your flooding sex

d) Sleeping in the front seat while their employers engage in wicked goings on deep inside the shadowy depths of a velvet-furnished brothel

e) Both a) and d)

Question 6.
Before succumbing to your irresistible temptation to initiate a forbidden Sapphic tryst in the servant's quarters with a fellow maid, you must first ensure that she is:

a) The disgraced daughter of a fallen noble family

b) A recent escapee from the Sultan's Harem

c) A virgin who learned the ways of oral love while the prisoner of rampaging savages on the sun-broiled steppes of a distant land

d) French

Question 7.
When administering a spanking to another female employee for some imagined transgression, you may use which of the following implements?

a) Her own filthy French objet-d'art, with which you just discovered the little slut disgracing herself in the pantry while plaintively whimpering the majordomo's name

b) A bundle of birch branches, prickly with the Autumn heat

c) Your naughty hand, no matter where it was last night, you little trollop. Probably plumbing the depths of that very same behind, slickened only by the juices of your own sex, eh what? Yes, I'm sure, there's a good girl. Now go to it!

d) All of the above

Question 8.
When receiving a spanking over your employer's knee, what is the proper response?

a) Flail your arms and legs uncontrollably while writhing in desperate resistance of the unchained beast this savage punishment has unleashed

b) Sob in inconsolable humiliation as the heretofore dormant volcano of your most bodily hungers erupts in a Gommorhic conflagration

c) Offer the gardener a blowjob

d) All of the above

Question 9.
That bulge in your employer's pants whenever he watches you dust is:

a) His rampaging manhood, swollen with the rabid humour of unchecked masculinity and beckoning to your quivering mouth, evoking such a longing as you have never experienced

b) His iron-stiff weapon, ripe and pulsating with the Australopithican thrill of a really good polo match, fox hunt or cricket game

c) Your whisk broom, which you doubtless left there when you offered him enthusiastic oral service after sweeping under the divan

d) French

Question 10.
When the lady of the house summons you to her bedchamber late in the evening and demands that you allow her to initiate you into the illicit rites of Lesbos, what is the proper response?

a) Quickly summon her husband so he can watch secretly from the shadowed confines of her wardrobe

b) Suggest that since such excesses are surely a mortal sin and will result in the damnation of your eternal soul, perhaps it would be best if she bound you with strips of cloth and stuffed your panties in your mouth

c) Both a and b

EXTRA CREDIT PART 1
Match the words in column A to their correct counterparts in
column B.

Column A	Column B
turgid	maid
sodden	amorist
heaving	rosebud
molten	clandestin
rhythmically throbbing	gardener
womanly	coquette
quivering	instructor
lust-crazed	quim
ardent	love-chasm
spanking-deprived	lance d'amour
desire-flushed	stable-boy
staggeringly-endowed	man-staff
oversexed	derriere
irresistible	sex-lips
silk-supple	pleasure-button
tempting	spendings
amoureux	bosom
orally-fixated	half-moons
well-savaged	juices

EXTRA CREDIT PART 2
When completing this exam, if time remains during the class period,
you should:

a) Realize that your final exam has left you victim to a curious
trembling in your nether regions, the murmur of a ravenous sex-
beast unleashed deep within your girlish soul

b) Surreptitiously sneak your hand under your skirt and realize
with dismay that you forgot to wear underwear today

c) Anticipate with lust-parted lips and fear-moist eyes your
failing score, knowing the instruction you receive from your betters,
though painful, will be for your own good

d) All of the above, and more....

About the Editor

Alison Tyler's erotic novels include *Learning To Love It*, *Strictly Confidential*, *Sweet Thing*, *Sticky Fingers*, and the upcoming *Something About Workmen*, all published by Black Lace Books. Two of her early novels, *The Blue Rose* and *The Virgin*, have recently been republished by Magic Carpet Books, along with a new erotic romance called *The ESP Affair*.

With Dante Davidson, she is the co-editor of the best-selling anthology *Bondage on a Budget* (Pretty Things Press) and the editor of *Naughty Stories from A to Z, Volumes 1 & 2* (PTP). Her short stories have appeared in anthologies including *Erotic Travel Tales I & II*, *Best Women's Erotica 2002 & 2003*, *Sweet Life 1 & 2*, and *Best Lesbian Erotica 1996* (all published by Cleis), and in *Best S/M Erotica* (Black Books), *Guilty Pleasures* (Black Books), *Sex Toy Tales* (Down There Press), *Midsummer Night's Dreams* (Masquerade), and *Wicked Words 4, 5, 6,* and *8* (Black Lace).

Ms. Tyler lives with her partner of eight years. They divide their time between a Paris flat and a Manhattan penthouse. At least, they do in their fantasies.

Juicy Erotica

Edited by
Alison Tyler

Bad Girl

Best Erotica
by Alison Tyler

Naughty Stories
from A to Z

Edited by Alison Tyler

Naughty Stories

from A to Z

Volume 2

Edited by Alison Tyler

Pretty Things Press, Inc.

Naughty Stories
From A to Z

Naughty Stories
From A to Z—Volume 2

Bondage on
a Budget

Bad Girl

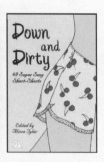

30 Erotic Tales
Written Just For Him

30 Erotic Tales
Written Just For Her

Down and Dirty

Juicy Erotica

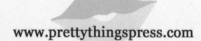

www.prettythingspress.com